MW01222791

SHOOFLY
PIE TO DIE

SHOOFLY
PIE TO DIE

JOSHUA QUITTNER
& MICHELLE SLATALLA

ST. MARTIN'S PRESS   NEW YORK

SHOOFLY PIE TO DIE. Copyright © 1992 by Joshua Quittner and Michelle Slatalla. All rights reserved. Printed in the United States of America. No part of this book may be used or reproduced in any manner whatsoever without written permission except in the case of brief quotations embodied in critical articles or reviews. For information, address St. Martin's Press, 175 Fifth Avenue, New York, N.Y. 10010

Production Editor: David Stanford Burr

Design by Dawn Niles

Library of Congress Cataloging-in-Publication Data

Quittner, Joshua.
  Shoofly pie to die / Joshua Quittner and Michelle Slatalla.
    p. cm.
  "A Thomas Dunne book."
  ISBN 0-312-06943-X
  I. Slatalla, Michelle. II. Title.
PS3567.U57S46 1992
813'.54—dc20

                                                              91-40345
                                                              CIP

First Edition: March 1992

10 9 8 7 6 5 4 3 2 1

SHOOFLY
PIE TO DIE

ONE

The plastic sack bulged like a garbage bag full of raked leaves that a cat had knocked over. Masking tape, once white but now crusted by brown goo, cinched it closed. Sam inspected the finger he had rubbed lightly against the tape. "Dried blood," he said. Don't jump to conclusions, he told himself.

Sara, at his side, peered at the bag. "Looks more like congealed blood," she said. "It's still kind of liquidy."

"Congealed blood," echoed Edward. "Maybe we better call the police?"

"Probably just a bag full of opossums or something that somebody stuck in the chest. Some joke," Sam said.

"Opossums?" Edward was only vaguely familiar with the word.

"Sam grew up in Iowa," Sara explained to Edward. "They have them there. They're kind of like big rats. I think."

"Chicago," Sam said.

"Wherever." Looks more like one big squishy thing than a bunch of little things, Sara thought.

Sam stood up, went briefly into the kitchen, and returned with a pair of tongs and a dishrag. These were not the tools one usually would need just to unwrap a bag full of dead mammals. Squatting with the tongs in one hand and the dishrag in the other, he carefully hoisted the bag upright. The tape, soaked through, loosened easily. Using the tongs, Sam methodically pulled it off in pieces, which he placed in a corner of the chest.

"Sam," Sara said.

"It's okay."

But it wasn't. The mouth of the bag gaped open, and there, suddenly, was the gnarled and bloodied stump of a human. So far, only the top half was visible. But where one would expect to see a head attached, there was ragged flesh, flecked with smaller bits of something that probably was bone, and a raw depth of slicked muscle and sinew.

"My God," moaned Edward. "Let's call the police. Do something . . . oh, God." This definitely was not part of his duties as a doorman. Carrying the chest up from the lobby was one thing; aiding and abetting was another.

"Edward, please," said Sara. This really was not the time for histrionics. Sam probed the torso with his tongs.

Edward, please? Edward thought. There's a dead body probably leaking blood all over the room and this woman acts like I just farted during her piano recital? But the doorman stayed put as Sam poked and prodded.

The blood was thick and caked around a wet, blackened collar.

"There's no head in there?" Sara asked.

2

"No head?" Edward said.

"No head," Sam confirmed. His tongs slipped the bag down farther, following the arms, which were stiffly crossed at the torso's waist.

"No hands, either," he said.

"No hands?" Edward said.

"No hands," said Sara. "Ritualistic? Any roosters or goat entrails?"

"Any roosters or goat . . . oh, God," said Edward.

Sam peeled the bag all the way down, patted it with the tongs and determined that it was now empty.

"Not that I can see. But it has no feet," Sam said.

"No feet?" Edward dropped back onto the couch. "No shit."

"None visible," Sara said.

The torso wore heavy black pants, held up by a single suspender. As Sam pulled the gummy bag carefully away, they could see that the fabric was rough and barely patterned, with a pinstripe so faint they could not say what color it was. The body, or what was left of it, was curled up like a boiled shrimp.

"Caucasian, male, tiny—could be a little old man—and it looks like his overcoat was fastened with hooks instead of buttons," Sam murmured reflexively.

"Sam, we're not on a story," Sara said. She shuddered to think that the arm Sam was touching so lightly—and the torso and the other stiff appendages attached to it—had ridden home with them (and with Baby! Would this be the beginning of years of expensive therapy, child psychiatrists, and tedious dream analysis?) from Pennsylvania to Manhattan, up the service elevator to the ninth floor and into their living room. The rug. Damn, stains.

"Sam, don't touch it anymore, please." Sam was gently pulling away the bag to see more. He stopped.

"Poor man," said Sara.

"Poor us," said Sam. He looked down at his hands and was surprised to see they were clean. He looked up at his wife. "I'll call the police."

"Poor me," said the puffy doorman, regaining his composure. "This is gonna cost you another twenty. A pallbearer I ain't."

TWO

Sam carried another tray out from the kitchen. "The world would be a better place if everybody cooked like you, Sammy," said Detective Stefan Stavropoulos. He wiped pastry off his mustache.

"I squeeze a little anchovy paste on the spinach before I stuff the phyllo," Sam confided. I am nuts, he thought, walking around a living room filled not with party guests but with cops holding paper napkins and hot hors d'oeurves. It is 2 A.M., and this is a murder investigation, and I am defrosting appetizers while Stavropoulos scrabbles around the cookie sheets like a hungry rooster. Nuts.

Instead of the usual New York cocktail chatter about how the homeless had completely taken over the Port Authority bus station or how an old lady in the next building had slipped on some frozen spit on the sidewalk, the conversation in the living room centered on the corpse, which still lay in the bag in the chest.

"Gimme a smile, Moe," said the police photographer, focusing his camera on the corpse.

"It is late. It is very late," Sam heard Sara say. He recognized the tone and almost pitied his interrogators.

Sara sat in the green chair. She picked listlessly at the overgrown cuticle of her right index finger.

She faced Detective Sergeant Evelyn Graber, a young police officer who, unlike their old friend Stavropoulos, was more adept at apprehending murderers than appreciating a really fine spanakopita. Graber's hair was a problem: It perched there, a greasy black octopus whose tentacles sucked at her shoulders. Graber took another sip from a thermos of black coffee she'd brought with her to the murder scene.

Graber consulted her notebook. "You said you went to Pennsylvania to review a restaurant for this newsletter you write. You had lunch. Where?"

"At the DeLuxe Diner. You already wrote it down. Crab cutlets and baked macaroni and cheese," Sara said. "Damn good macaroni and cheese. Check page six of your notes."

Graber knew very well what her notes said. Her eyes continued to pin Sara down, taking in the dark hair, the black stretch pants that could have been stolen off Laura Petry, the bitten nails.

"This newsletter."

"The Thin Man," Sara said. "You wrote it down on page three of your notes."

"Diet food?" Graber asked.

"Hardly," Sara said. "It's a play on words. A joke. Do you know what a joke is?"

Graber knew very well what a joke was. In theory.

"So this *Thin Man,* it's a newsletter about regional American food, and you're working on an issue about Pennsylvania Dutch cooking?"

"Gee, things haven't changed a bit since the first time we went over this, two hours ago."

Stavropoulos, who had no real interest in murder investigations, followed Sam back into the kitchen. "This newsletter ever falls flat, I got something might interest you," he said.

"Not the doughnut store," Sam said.

"New one."

"Bagel store?"

"Cat's pajamas." Stavropoulos beamed. "Sara designs them. We sell them. Everybody's got a cat, right? People are nuts about their pets."

"Hmmm."

"For an extra ten bucks we sell them a little nightcap to go with the pj's."

"Uh-huh."

"And we design a really cool box. That's all these things are, packaging. Like pet rocks. Screaming yellow zonkers."

"Stefan, wait it out. A couple more years and you'll have your pension," Sam said, greasing a baking sheet.

"Yeah, but I get bored," Stavropoulos said. He wandered off to find out if the photographer owned a cat.

In the living room Graber was unconcerned at the lateness of the hour. A sour disposition and too much coffee, not lack of sleep, was to blame for the pinched face and squint she trained on Sara. "Now, let me get this straight. First you said you decided to come back home because the baby got sick, then you said it was because of the snow." Her ballpoint scratched accusingly in her notebook. "So which is it?"

"Both. Page eleven of your notes."

"Why did you go into this store, this Farm Salvage, in the first place?"

"Because it didn't say 'antiques' on the sign."

"The owner—what was his name?"

"We don't know. He was tall and thin . . . and sweaty, even though the heat was barely on," Sara suddenly remembered.

The police photographer hunkered down in front of Sara to take a shot of the chest and its contents. Almost before the flash faded, he had moved forty-five degrees to set up the same shot again. He asked Stavropoulos to hold a yardstick alongside the corpse.

Flipping through her notes, Graber said, "First you said you were in Pennsylvania to review the diner, and then you said it was because you were going to a smorgasbord for supper—which, incidentally, you never went to—so which is it?"

Irked more by Graber's apparent obliviousness to the ugliness of nude-colored panty hose (hers were pilled, for God's sake) than by her nit-picking questions, Sara said in a low voice more menacing than a scream: "Frankly, it's a wonder you catch any murderers in this city if you spend all your time harassing innocent witnesses. We have been over this a dozen times. You've got the body of what looks like an old man. Somebody doesn't want you to identify him. Somebody in Pennsylvania. You really should be talking to the guy who sold us the chest instead of breaking our shoes. We would like to go to sleep."

Her opinion was seconded by an exasperated wail from the nursery.

A pair of technicians from the crime lab pulled off their rubber gloves and popped two little spinach pies into their mouths. The hair samples from the bedroom and bathroom floors that they had carefully stashed in little plastic bags would be examined under a high-powered microscope alongside fibers scraped from the victim's clothes. Just in case. They signed out with the plainclothes sentry at the door.

"This is not that difficult," Graber said. She crossed one nude-colored leg over the other. "If you're telling the truth." Uh-oh, thought Sam from the kitchen. She's gone too far. "It's a long time since I burst out crying because policemen didn't like me," Sara said. When Sara started quoting from *The Maltese Falcon,* Sam sensed danger. He came into the living room and saw Sara had opened the door to the hall. "Maybe, if you have more questions after you interview the store owner, we could talk again," she said, pointedly starting to clear away the napkins and crumbs abandoned by the photographer, the lab techs, the assistant district attorney, the assistant medical examiner, and the officer on doorman duty. Stavropoulos chose to hang onto his napkin; another batch of pies was still heating up.

"Weird," Stavropoulos said. They all turned to look at him. He pointed with the yardstick. "This mook must've been a midget."

The assistant medical examiner looked up from the notes he was writing. "What do you mean?"

"Nothing. It just looks like the little guy's got to be a hunchback or something. And his arms are awful short, even without hands. Weird." Stavropoulos went off to forage for spinach pies.

The assistant ME put down his pen and pulled a tape measure from his bag. "You know, he could be right."

"What do you mean?" Graber snapped. Her coffee-marinated bowels tightened at the sickening thought that Stavropoulos had done it again.

"The torso is only about as long as a ten-year-old child's. The limbs—what's left of them—are severely stunted. I think we could be dealing with a dwarf," the assistant ME said. "Not a midget really, though. There's a medical difference."

Stavropoulos shrugged.

"Well, let me know as soon as you verify," Graber said,

her expressionless squint trained on the body that was being zipped into a black rubber bag. She smiled for the first time. "Is that your baby crying?" she asked, and followed the corpse from the room.

"Is that her breath or did someone leave the garbage chute open?" Sara whispered.

"Listen, you guys, nobody thinks you did it. We just got a job to do," Stavropoulos said. On his way out he stopped and smiled helpfully over his shoulder. "But you really ought to get a lawyer."

THREE

The sign they had seen that afternoon had not said much. Just FURNITURE: TURN RIGHT.

"Does that sign mean there's stuff for sale, or does it mean that all the furniture that comes driving down this road is being ordered to make a right turn?" Sara asked.

"You sound like a copy editor," Sam said. "I married a copy editor. Great."

"Sweetie, would a copy editor be out in broad daylight? No, they only work at night. Would a copy editor be driving in a car in the middle of the country? No, they hate fresh air. Would a copy editor be trying to convince her husband to browse through secondhand furniture? No, they rarely find spouses," Sara said. "Don't even joke about such things in front of the i-n-f-a-n-t. We don't want her to develop a fetish for tortured g-r-a-m-m-a-r."

Like most obsessions, Sara's bias against copy editors had gained momentum over the years, fueled by a series of unpleasant experiences. Once, in their previous life as newspaper reporters, acting on another misguided recommendation from their editor, Sam and Sara had invited a couple of copy editors over for dinner. They appreciate good food, just like you and me, Max Goldberg had lied. And they might remember a little gesture of friendliness the next time they're deciding whether to screw up your prose so badly that readers call in for a translation.

By the time the elevator carrying the copy editors had reached the ninth floor, the dinner guests had edited the sign, "Capacity: 10 By Order of Fire Marshal," and subbed in "Authorities in New York City, an urban area of New York State, recommend that fewer than 11 adult persons, at most, occupy the premises of this Otis elevator at any one time." The dinner had not been a success.

Copy editors, in fact, had been the top item on the list Sam and Sara had drawn up under the heading "Why Quit Job" as they weighed the possibility of rash behavior, trying to decide whether to walk away from their video display terminals and health insurance benefits to start their own business. "Please, please," wept Max, hugging Sara's ankles, reaching out to stroke Sam's scuffed loafers (somehow, this is how they always remembered the scene), "don't leave us. The paper needs you."

"Copy editors," Sara and Sam had replied. Max wailed. They walked.

There the fantasy ended, and they learned that free-lance writing was not a particularly lucrative way to make a living. Sure, they sold a steady supply of "Inside New York" stories to the usual glitzy city magazines: "Where the Famous Eat,"

"What the Famous Eat," "Why the Poor Are Dying on Sidewalks in Front of Restaurants Frequented by the Famous." Sam and Sara's recent Pulitzer Prize, awarded as it was for a series on the New York restaurant industry, had given them near-celebrity status for a while. No matter that their newspaper articles had focused on abuses and fraud in the industry; their stories now involved such investigations as who first thought of stuffing agnolotti with chopped jicama—and why, for God's sake.

They had quickly tired of worrying about how they would pay the rent if today's mail contained no checks. And they had gotten bored with cranking out the stuff, particularly in the bitchy style that seemed to be the sole dialect magazine editors understood.

On the advice of a friend, they wrote a travel piece about feast days among the Pueblo Indians in northern New Mexico. They had so much fun with that that they did another story on pit beef in Maryland. Working on those articles enabled them to focus on two of the three things they enjoyed most—eating and traveling.

Then Sara came up with the idea of a food newsletter while she was shaving her legs.

"Sam, it makes sense. Alyssa told me about these people who put out a newsletter on theater and netted a hundred grand a year. We don't even know anybody who goes to the theater."

"What a great scam," Sam said from the tub. "Think of the tax deductions. We'll write off the Range Rover."

Now, they set their own hours, spent as much time with Baby as they wanted, traveled, and ate their fill. The money was decent, better than they had been making before.

And no copy editors, thought Sara. She sighed and settled deeper into the ergonomically cushioned passenger seat. That comfortable drowsiness that so often follows a big dish of baked macaroni and cheese had enveloped Sara, who normally wouldn't be susceptible to such feelings. Because normally she would not think of ordering baked macaroni and cheese—what, risk exposure to limply overcooked noodles under a floury cheese paste?—in a diner. But the DeLuxe Diner was no typical roadside joint. Sam and Sara had, in fact, planned the entire Eastern Pennsylvania issue of *The Thin Man* around a trip to the DeLuxe, where the owner turned out a crab cutlet so delicious that first-time customers had been known to weep in startled gratitude upon taking a bite.

From lunch at the diner, in West Reading, they had planned to drive south, into Lancaster County. The idea was to end up, by suppertime, at the Shady Maple smorgasbord just outside Blue Ball. The reputation of the indigenous Pennsylvania Dutch cooking at the Shady Maple—corn relish, deep-fried pineapple, and just about any dish you could think of containing pork—was a powerful lure.

But as usual, they arrived far too early, with a good four hours to kill. The gray afternoon sky was dark even for January. "I'm still full," Sam said.

"Let's go someplace that doesn't sell antiques, then. Maybe we could find a morris chair."

Sam eased the Range Rover down a narrow dirt lane, guarded by a coopful of scruffy chickens. The road led to a sagging barn with a big, hand-lettered sign that said, "Farm Salvage." Through the open back doors they could see merchandise—potential bargains all—and a couple of men, crouched beside a stack of end tables, as if taking inventory.

An hour or so of digging through piles of used clothes, rusted farm tools, and back issues of *Arizona Highways* was just the sort of exercise they had been looking for. Just the way to work off lunch and build an appetite for supper. It would take their minds off the deadline that loomed.

Sam turned off the ignition and grabbed his parka from the backseat. He stroked its collar: This was no ordinary coat.

14

In an earthy wardrobe of flannel shirts, worn corduroys, and beaten cowboy boots, the red parka stood out like a seashell on the beach. It wasn't often that Sam became fixated on an article of clothing. The objects he loved best were his pots and pans and his cooking gear. Now and then he collected some ridiculous piece of electronic equipment, like the computerized pocket diary he mooned over for weeks, then discarded in favor of a cordless phone that made local calls sound as if they were conducted via satellite.

But when Sam had seen the waxed linen parka in a catalog, he had become obsessed with owning it. Maybe it was because it came with its own toys. (The owner was urged to apply a coating of wax from a little can. "An early form of waterproofing," the instruction booklet—a coat with an instruction booklet?—explained.) Maybe it was because of all the hidden pockets. "I can keep my microcorder in it. I can store my electronic diary in the game pouch," Sam had said to Sara. She didn't need to be convinced. Any large purchase he made gave her license to run up a complementary tab at Saks.

Sam withdrew a baby bottle of juice from a double-secret pocket under the right armpit. He uncinched Baby from the uncomfortable web of straps and braces that would protect her from death in a head-on collision ("Nice car seat," Sam told the glaring infant). He lifted her out and she coughed. Not just her usual pay-attention-to-me cough, Sam thought. "Come here, puss face," Sara said, feeling her forehead. "Not warm."

"Yet," said Sam.

"I married the Voice of Doom." The three of them treaded across the makeshift gravel parking lot into Farm Salvage.

It smelled like pig. But nothing seemed to be rooting around the aisles of chipped plates and rotting books, not even the two men who had been crouched in the aisle. They had disappeared, and in their place Sara saw the pine chest.

It was, by far, the best piece of furniture that she could

see. It sat next to a moldy dressmaker's mannequin, behind a shelf of deteriorating detective paperbacks. The long, low chest was painted milk-blue and stencilled, with a sturdy handle at each end. Curious, Sara sat Baby on the cement floor, next to a box of buttons, and tried to lift the lid.

"Stuck?" Sam asked. He tugged. "Too bad," he said. "Could have stored a lot of old reporter's notebooks in there."

"Could be warped, or it could just need some fiddling," Sara said. "I wonder how much it costs."

"Fifty dollars," said a man who appeared suddenly from the back of the shop. He looked to be about thirty, tall and thin and with black hair—hair that seemed all the darker framing a face whiter than a sushi bar squid. "Fifty dollars unless you want it shipped. And we don't ship. You don't live around here?"

"That's right . . ." said Sara.

"New York plates. Saw them when you drove in."

"Got a key for this thing?" asked Sam.

"Nope. As is."

"Hmmm."

The man said: "If I had a key for it, I'd charge you seventy-five."

"We'll take it," said Sara.

The man loaded the chest as an anemic snowflake fluttered onto Sara's nose. Baby sneezed. "Looks like winter's finally here," said the man. "Have a nice drive back." He returned to the barn.

Baby coughed. "Sam," said Sara.

"Say no more," said Sam. The Shady Maple would have to wait; they were going home. He nosed the Rover back onto the road.

Had they looked back, they would have seen someone turn off the lights, pull shut the big barn doors, and flip the sign in the window to CLOSED.

FOUR

Baby was drafting a writ of habeas corpus. Her favorite stuffed animal, the Penguin, was nailing the crib onto a chair on top of a rickety table. The stack of furniture climbed to the rafters at Farm Salvage. Baby, imprisoned in the crib, didn't notice the swaying; she was due in court in an hour to plead her case. Sara saw the pendulum of furniture swing in ever-widening arcs, but she couldn't help. She was swimming in a stockpot full of macaroni and cheese. Penguin kept pounding.

The hammering got louder, and Sara sat up, shook off sleep, and looked around the bedroom. It was Monday morning. It was sunny. The Penguin was in the corner of the crib, and the noise came not from the nursery, but the kitchen, where Baby seemed intent on denting all the expensive pots that her father owned.

Sam looked up when Sara stumbled in. "Too bad we don't work for the paper anymore," he said.

"Good morning to you too, Dutch."

"Sorry. I didn't sleep so well last night. I was trying to figure this out."

He sat at the big oak table, patiently spooning choo-choo trainfuls of peas into the tunnel Baby obligingly made of her mouth. The infant was cheerfully pounding a pot lid against the tray of her high chair.

"And?"

"And I was thinking how it's too bad we aren't reporters anymore. This is one murder story where we wouldn't have to use 'police said' in the lead. We've got the information first-hand."

"We don't have enough information to make sense."

Sara poured herself a cup of coffee (the beans were air-mailed from Graffeo, in San Francisco) and took up her position as Sam's assistant at the cutting board beneath the hanging rack of Calphalon pots. She began to dice the Grade 1 yellowfin tuna Sam had just bought at Citarella on Broadway near 75th.

"Since when do newspaper stories have to make sense?" Sam said. "Who: headless midget wearing pants with one broken suspender. What: murder victim. When: sometime Sunday. Where: somewhere in the Keystone State. How: gruesomely."

Gruesomely was not an adverb Sam used lightly, not since his first day on his first job as a cop reporter. Drop by and we'll get acquainted, suggested Dr. Jack Ridley, the Cuyahoga County medical examiner. The morgue had been kind of cold, the white tile floor and walls kind of clammy, when Sam walked in. The Ripper, bent over a body, had straightened, holding a fork with red, goopy intestine twirled around it. A fat gob of blood spattered on the white tile as Ridley ate a long strand.

When Sam came to, the Ripper was sheepish. "Stuck my lunch down in there," he said. "The wife always sends spaghetti on Thursdays."

Now Sara wiped the blade of her knife. "But we don't know why he was killed," she said.

"Why is not the problem. Why us is the problem."

Sara turned on the front burner of the Jenn-Air stove, adjusted the flame to low, and quickly ran sheets of nori over the fire to crisp them. She spread the papery seaweed on the cutting board and onto each piece dabbed a thin layer of rice, some diced tuna, and a line of green radish sprouts. She rolled each nori and cut the logs into bite-sized pieces.

"And we really don't know who, either," Sara said. "Or anything else, for that matter."

"Start with where. That's probably easiest."

"I'd say Lancaster County is a safe guess. Probably the store. If that's where he was cut up, the cops will find a bloody back room when they get there." Sara poured soy sauce into a little saucer and placed it next to a mound of wasabe on their lacquered sushi tray.

"I wonder how much blood we're really talking about," Sam said, settling a still-sticky Baby into her tot rod and following the careening infant across the hardwood floor into the living room.

"Buckets and buckets, I would imagine," Sara said to herself, expertly carving a radish into a rose to garnish the neat rows of tekka maki that marched across the tray.

"Actually not," Sam said, coming back into the kitchen with an oversized forensic text. It looked like a book you would find on a coffee table. But instead of Andy Warhol's pop art, this book had photos of such things as defense wounds inflicted in attempts to grab a knife, and crescent-shaped injuries to the leg produced by the flat end of a claw hammer.

Sam read aloud: " 'If dismemberment is sustained postmortem, relatively little bleeding will occur and the edges of the wounds will appear slightly dry.' "

"That would explain why he didn't leak in the car or on the rug."

"But that doesn't explain how he died."

"Or where or when. Sam, do you think we bought the chest with the dwarf already in it, or could somebody have put it in when we stopped for supper in New Jersey?"

"We bought it. At no extra charge. I can't see somebody slipping a bloody corpse into our car without our knowledge while we were peacefully eating cheeseburgers in a diner. Besides, the thing was locked. Somebody with the key—and a body—followed us to a diner in New Jersey? Too farfetched."

"If it was there at Farm Salvage, that either means Squidly put it in, or else the chest was already doing double duty as a coffin when he bought it."

"I don't think the body could have been there too long, Frenchie." He popped a maki into his mouth. He flipped through the textbook. "From the amount of rigor mortis, I'd estimate he'd been dead under twelve hours."

"How are the cops going to identify him without his head, his hands, and his feet?"

Sam read from a second book he had opened on the table. " 'Primary means of identifying homicide victims is skeletal structure of the skull.' Good luck."

"Maybe somebody didn't want him to be identified."

"Clearly."

"Maybe there's a missing person's report."

"Maybe. Wonder how long he's been missing."

"So how are we going to figure out who the guy is and why he ended up dead in a chest we bought?"

"We aren't, Sara. The cops are. The cops. They eat this stuff up. They get paid to do it. We don't."

"Come on, Sam, somebody sticks us with a stiff and you don't even want to follow it up? I want my chest back!"

"Sara, we got out of the business. We don't investigate anymore. Except food. We investigate food very thoroughly. Food is fun. Murder is not. We don't have to do unfun things anymore. I thought that was the point of starting this newsletter."

"I suppose you're right."

Baby skittered back into the kitchen and rammed, full throttle, into one of the thick, solid legs of the table.

"Bless you, Gustav Stickley, for designing infantproof furniture," Sara murmured, swiping at Baby's mouth with a napkin.

"Still, I wonder what killed him. It would be sporting to at least know the cause of death." Sam headed for the living room.

Sara could hear him flipping through old reporter's notebooks, looking for the scribblings he had saved from the time he enrolled, undercover, in the police academy.

"Mommy and Daddy are going to solve a murder," she whispered to Baby.

The banner still drooped across the arched doorway to the living room. Red, blue, green, silver, and gold letters spelling WELCOME HOME. The old man sighed, grabbed his hat, tightened his scarf, and went out onto the stoop, hugging the concrete banister as he navigated the icy steps.

Even in winter Carroll Gardens is alive, he thought. Schoolchildren raced to a bus stop, and the old man smiled at them. He stopped for a paper at Cappy's newsstand, and Cappy gave him a look. The old man shook his head.

"Still no news?"

"*Niente,* nothing," said the old man. He paid for his *Post.* It was a bad sign, his son not coming home as planned. It was not good, Dommy not calling. There hadn't even been a letter. Then again, from the moment Dommy had been born, there were no good signs, starting with the frown from the doctor when the baby had come. A midget, a dwarf. Who knew why? The old man had always thought it had something to do with bad diet, something Maria had eaten. Maybe the Milanese food that time, who knows?

He walked slowly past the Imperial Fruit Market, which had a plastic tent out front to protect the oranges and grapes and broccoli from the cold. He could do this walk blind, which he wasn't yet, thank God. The travel agency was next, with that receptionist with the legs sitting by the window, and then La Sicilia II, a pizza place that sounded more like a penny arcade, what with those video games in there. And then he was at his own business, The DeMedici Barber Shop, Marcello Calvesi, prop., which he had run for the past fifty years.

The old man hung his overcoat on the metal rack and pulled on a white smock, one of three, freshly laundered, that hung there. He sighed and sat on the brown vinyl couch and, with a flourish, whipped open the paper, wetting his right index finger and turning the page, waiting for the first customer.

"My dear friend, Frankie," the old man said as the bells jingled on the door about five hours later and his first customer walked in. Business was unusually brisk for a Monday.

"Afternoon, Marcello," said Frankie Tartaglia. They were of an age, these two. Classmates at St. Anthony's, their fathers had known each other. Tartaglia had been a salesman for one of the bigger knitwear firms, retired years ago, something the old man could have done, too, had he been so inclined. But he didn't retire—what would he do? Maria was long dead, his children had moved away. Except Dommy, who had "moved" upstate.

Tartaglia sat in the chair, and the barber took up his place behind him.

"Any word from Dominic?"

"No."

The old man pinned a towel around Tartaglia's neck. He picked up his scissors.

"You call the cops?"

"For what?"

"For what? For what? You got a missing person on your hands is for what."

"He's an ex-con. The cops don't care for an ex-con."

"Mama, will you listen to this fucking guy?" Tartaglia said for effect.

"Don't move your head." The barber was doing some inside work, clipping the bristly hairs from Tartaglia's ears.

"Ex-con or no, he's a citizen, he's got a right to be looked for same as you and me. He told you he'd be coming home last Friday?"

"He called. I want to drive up there and get him and he tells me no. Don't bother. He'll take the bus. So fine, I say. Take the bus. You come home, you stay with me, and it'll be okay. Does he come home? No."

"You should call the police. It's been ten days and not a word."

"Ehh." The old man waved his hand in disgust. In silence he finished trimming his friend's gray hair and brushed off the back of his neck. He refused to meet his look in the mirror.

After he put on his overcoat, Tartaglia said simply, "You got an obligation as his father," and left.

The old man muttered and picked up the *Post* again, flipping it open. But when the bells stopped jangling on the door and Tartaglia's dirty brown coat was out of sight, Old Man Calvesi picked up the receiver from the rotary telephone and dialed "O."

"I want to report a missing person," he told the operator.

FIVE

The fisherman had chipped a hole into the frozen surface that covered the reservoir. He had been angling for about an hour, without success, when he looked up and recognized a tall, pale man standing on the shore. The fisherman waved to the man, who made his way cautiously out to the middle of the lake, slipping on the ice just enough to betray the fact that he was unused to such endeavors.

A carriage, pulled by a pair of panting black horses, clopped down the road that led to the reservoir, then veered off down a smaller road and disappeared, with its Amish family, into the countryside.

"You were late," the pale man said. "I was here at noon. You weren't."

"I was busy," the fisherman said, staring into the inky water.

"I want my money," the man said. "Now."

"The money was a down payment." The fisherman avoided the man's eyes.

"The deal is off," the man said. "I was double-crossed."

"I was double-crossed, too," the fisherman whined. "How do you think I feel?"

"Scared?"

"Of course."

A chill wind blew in off the rocky hills that ringed the lake. Only a few thick-skinned anglers were left on the ice, and most were packing up rods and tackle boxes, or already trekking toward parked cars on the far bank. It would soon be dark.

The fisherman said: "I think I can still deliver."

"You think you can deliver?" the man said. He reached into the fisherman's tackle box and retrieved a small fish hook. He pulled the barb across the soft flesh between his thumb and index finger, watching curiously as a bead of blood welled up. He made a fist.

"I'm working on it," the fisherman said. "I know I can."

"Bullshit."

"I need a few days."

"Bullshit. I want my hundred and fifty grand back. Today."

"Why don't you give me a week and you'll have what you want?" the fisherman said. "What have you got to lose?"

"What the fuck have you done with my money?"

"Listen, if you want your piddly down payment back, you may have it. However, no one's interests are served in that case. Not yours, because you do not get what you're looking for. Not mine, because I do not get paid. And I desperately want to be paid, especially now that I will not have to split my profit with someone else. I suppose I should thank you for that."

The fisherman could already see the fat moon hanging in the sky. He hated night fishing in the winter. He snapped shut his tackle box.

"One week," the man said. "And you'd better fucking come through."

"One week," the fisherman said. "You know where to reach me." He walked off, leaving the pale man staring at his own ghostly reflection in the smooth depths. A drop of blood splashed into the hole, and a trout rose to snap.

Graber gazed happily at the photos before her.

Sara's face looked puffy and bruised, and Sam's skin was rockier than the lunar surface in the driver's license pictures that Graber was faxing to Lancaster County.

They were the typically unflattering photos that the Motor Vehicles Department specializes in. In the world populated by civil servants masquerading as photographers (whose artistic exhortations run to "Stand on the line" and "Look straight at the camera"), all female subjects look like victims of domestic violence. All males look like victims of smoke inhalation.

On a typical Monday Graber would not have seen these photos. She would have prevailed upon Stavropoulos to do the tedious work, the querying of Motor Vehicles, the faxing of documents. But Detective Stavropoulos had floated off around ten-thirty, muttering something vague about a coffee break—Graber did not believe in coffee breaks—and had not returned. Three hours later Graber was beginning to worry. Not about her partner, of course, but about the success of this case.

Although Graber's stellar record in the homicide bureau (fourteen cases: fourteen confessions) belied her youth, it also made her uneasy. That phenomenal string of solved murders was due, in large part, to the teamwork of Graber and Stavropoulos. Not that Stavropoulos had any inkling. He just kept wandering through life, in and out of crime scenes, ruminating on the possibility of changing careers. But as he was musing about raising a stand of black walnut trees (fifty years to maturity but worth their weight in caviar) or breeding miniature Vietnamese pigs (they make lovely house pets, and the piglets sell for $3,000 apiece, assuming you have a mommy miniature Vietnamese pig and a daddy miniature Vietnamese pig), he had an uncanny way of accidentally noticing the unnoticed. It might be a monogrammed pen the murderer had dropped in a corner. It might be a downward smear of blood by the light switch indicating that the husband couldn't possibly have found his wife's body like that in a dark room.

Or it might be the fact that a dead body belonged to a dwarf.

These observations would have been very distressing to Graber—if he had known the import of his utterances. But Stavropoulos, being Stavropoulos, was always more interested in whether a murder victim's line of work might prove lucrative than in apprehending his killer. The gleaming little facts he blurted were gifts bestowed unknowingly on his partner, who usually managed to take the credit before anyone else realized the source of her inspiration.

But since the source seemed to be taking an inordinately long coffee break today, Graber had been a little short on ideas. Until the phone call.

And now she had a possible victim and two suspects. Two suspects that she desperately wanted to do the blue jackets on.

She stared at the driver's license photos of Sam and Sara

until her eyes narrowed. Then she squinted at the computer screen that still displayed the vital statistics on file (Amstel, Sara; Date of birth: 07/11/56, Eyes: Black; Height: 5 ft. Popkin, Samuel; Date of birth: 10/12/54; Eyes: Brown; Height: 5 ft 10 in). The fax machine swallowed and then spit out the pages like undigested watermelon seeds.

That picture of her is too flattering, Graber thought idly, picking up the copy of Sara's photo, blackening one incisor with her felt tip. And I don't think she's that tall. Pip-squeak. Graber did not like short people. Dead or alive. Or married people, for that matter, because they so often seemed more interested in each other than in getting their work done.

Graber thought she was tall. She had formed that opinion in the seventh grade, when the embarrassment of adolescence had led her to affect an ungainly slouch that she had not been able to shake, even years after the hormones that blurred her teenage image in the mirror had subsided. In her mind, she would always tower above everyone else, the girl who had achieved adult height when most of her classmates still resembled Snow White's sidekicks.

With the slouch Graber in motion evoked a sailboat listing uneasily to one side in the hands of an inexpert sailor. Her feet arrived in a room half a beat before her head, a circumstance that Stavropoulos considered a temporary dispensation from God that enabled him to prepare for her hair before he actually had to look at it.

On the desk beside her was a list: Call ME, Call lab, Fax pix, Why no luggage to Pa? The first three items were checked off.

She heard Lt. Harry Erbatz clomping down the hall in his thick-soled loafers long before he stuck his head around the edge of the door and said, "Your preliminary report is very complete. As usual."

"Thanks," Graber said.

She looked up quizzically, and the dreaded Stavropoulos popped his head around the corner of the door. "Hi, Evvie," he said sheepishly. He was mouthing a plastic fork, something he liked to bend the way other people fatigue paper clips.

"Where have you been, Stavropoulos?" Graber took care not to hiss in front of Erbatz.

"Uh, lunch?" Stavropoulos said.

"Lunch?"

"Yes, Evelyn, we had lunch," Erbatz said. "The Little Shanghai. You should try it sometime."

"I am not a lunch person," she said briskly. It was well known at One Police Plaza that Evelyn Graber last had lunch six years ago when she was invited to a Meet-the-Boss luncheon with the commissioner.

"I asked Stavropoulos for an update on the midget murder," Erbatz said. "I understand from the ME's office that his observations at the crime scene were very useful. I also understand there was a bit of animosity between you and the witnesses."

His eyes swept the glassed-in cubicle, cataloging the scuffed walls, the dusty desktop where the computer terminal sat, the sensible metal chair Graber occupied. She seemed not to notice that the thermostat was set for 60 degrees.

"I was going to come in and tell you all about it, I wanted to give you a full report, Lieutenant. But I had to get these pictures to the Lancaster County sheriff's office as soon as possible," Graber said. "So we can verify fast and, I hope, get this cleared up."

"You need to send photos before Lancaster will go to a potential murder scene?"

"Actually, Lieutenant, I wanted to send them the full package as fast as possible. It seemed to be more efficient."

"Graber, you don't actually suspect them, do you? Two well-known yuppie food critics?"

Graber smiled quickly. This was going to be fun, she thought. "Just because they get invited to all the right parties doesn't necessarily mean they can't be criminals."

"Come on, Graber."

"Give me a chance," she said. She rooted around on her desk and flipped a call-in report to Erbatz. "Dominic Calvesi's father just called in a report. Calvesi's been missing since last week, when he got out of jail."

"So? For a midget, he's a pretty tough guy, and so is the crowd he hung around with."

"Calvesi was tough—for his size. Quite a coincidence," Graber said. "Our headless corpse, in fact, could fit into one of his tailor-made Giorgio Armani cutoff suits."

"Assuming it had hands and feet," Stavropoulos said.

"Interesting, Evelyn," Erbatz said at last. "But extremely farfetched."

Graber didn't react.

"Lancaster have any MPs?"

"Nobody missing they know of. They're checking neighboring jurisdictions."

"So how are you pursuing this Calvesi theory?"

"Sing Sing is checking for his medical records."

"Well, keep on it, Graber. And make sure you get those photos up to Lancaster. I'm sure this is their murder, not ours. Whacking Calvesi. Very cute, Evelyn. Any luck and you'll be stamping this file 'Case Closed' by tomorrow."

He knew Graber loved to use her "Case Closed" stamp. Almost as much as she liked her "Classified Documents" stamp. At least she'd stopped using the ink pad to practice fingerprinting herself. "Keep me informed, Graber."

She listened to Erbatz's loafers walking away down the hallway.

"Can I get you some coffee, Evvie?" Stavropoulos asked. She said no and shooed him away. She had business to attend to. Graber picked up the phone and called a reporter she knew—something she did about as often as she ate lunch.

SIX

The following morning a skinny man in a clown suit and rainbow fright wig got onto the IRT at 72nd Street. As the subway doors closed (more or less) behind him, he put a megaphone to his lips, and shrieked over the howl of the train: "Attention! All money collected will be used to send inner-city children to Camp Krishna, a nonprofit summer camp in the Adirondacks! Thank you and have a nice day!" Then he pressed a button on the side of the megaphone, unleashing a discordant rendition of "Merrily We Roll Along." He fumbled for a plastic pail that was a fifth full of change, and slowly staggered the length of the subway car, pushing the bucket under the bloodshot eyes of the bleary, morning straphangers.

Stanley Smith, Esq., did not hear or see the skinny man in the clown suit. Stanley Smith, Esq., was about as absorbed as he could get. The object of his absorption was a story on page three of Tuesday's *New York Newsday.*

He read:

The two food critics shared a Pulitzer Prize for investigative journalism six years ago, for a series exposing widespread corruption among many of the city's health inspectors who monitor restaurants, and revealing mob dominance of the eating industry.

Their stories resulted in the indictment of dozens of high-ranking city employees, as well as Dominic "The Muscle" Calvesi, a midget who is a reputed organized crime figure convicted of extorting money from restaurant owners.

Calvesi was recently released from jail after serving four years, according to a spokesman for the State Board of Corrections.

The two reporters subsequently left journalism to publish a newsletter about American regional cuisine.

A Stanley Smith absorbed in his reading is a Stanley Smith not to be trifled with. Smith's powers of concentration had been legendary at Harvard, where he insisted on studying for his first-year finals while listening to every album Frank Zappa ever recorded, in chronological sequence, on stereo headphones turned up full blast. So when the mutant with the rainbow hair put the pail under Smith's nose, Smith was understandably startled.

"Get the fuck away from me," Smith said into the pail. The panhandler glared, then moved on. Smith watched him, then glanced across the filthy, soda-slicked aisle of the No. 2 train and caught the eye of a young woman in a strangely shaped hat. Smith smiled. The woman smiled. Smith looked closely at the woman's hat. It was not a hat after all; it was a baloney sandwich. With mustard.

Smith turned back to his story.

Police have not released the name of the victim. The body bore no identification. Authorities, who said it will take at least a week to complete forensic tests on the chest, the plastic bags encasing the victim, and his clothes, would not rule out the possibility that the body is Calvesi's.

Police say the victim found in the couple's Riverside Drive apartment had been dead between 12 and 24 hours.

Authorities would not say where they believed the murder occurred.

That was an ominous kicker. Luckily for Smith, he finished reading the story as the subway reached the 96th Street station. Too often he would get lost in his reading and end up in the Bronx. As he left the car, the woman in the baloney sandwich looked up at him as if to say something. Smith hurried past. He took the crowded escalator up to Broadway, where a blast of New York winter raked his face.

Smith tentatively took a sniff, and found the scent he was looking for: Frying eggs. Watercress. Bacon. An omelette? He imagined a Merry Melody cartoon, the odor of cooking food now a smoky finger, tickling his nose, leading him right up Broadway. At 101st Street he turned west, following the smell, which was getting stronger, into a prewar apartment building, past a small doorman, and into an elevator.

He was salivating as he opened the door to 9P.

"Delicious, Dutch," Sara said, taking a bite of the bacon and watercress omelette without looking up from *The New*

York Times. "Did you by any chance put a little anchovy paste in this, too?"

"Oh, it's just a little of this, a little of that," Sam said, placing a plate in the oven to warm. "Only the cops can squeeze my secret ingredients from me. Good morning, Stanley."

"Apparently the police are being coy," Sara said, looking up from the newspaper. "Killing midget hit men. Marvelous. Good morning, Stanley."

"I hope they don't think we were in cahoots with Edward and killed him on the living room floor," Sam said.

"Very impressive. From writing newspaper articles to appearing in them. You two must be very proud," Smith said.

Sara looked appraisingly at the balding and bulky man in an ill-fitting blue suit, the same suit he had been wearing more or less daily since going into private practice with a downtown law firm three years ago. "Do you think we need a lawyer, Stanley? Everyone else does," she said.

"Can I get you some breakfast, Smith?" Sam asked.

"No, thanks, I just ate. But if you have any Diet Coke, I could go for one." It would be his third since shaving. He sat down at the table and started cooing at Baby, who was ensconced in a high chair resplendent with a translucent coating of mashed banana and applesauce.

Loosening his collar, Smith exhibited the sweaty discomfort most often found in fifteen-year-old boys sent off to their first semester of prep school.

"I think you guys could use some professional advice," Smith said, picking at Sara's omelette. "Hmmm, is this anchovy?"

His stained tie, mismatched socks, and sick-puppy eyes belied his high-powered education and six-year stint as one of the most successful prosecutors working for the U.S. Attorney in the Eastern District. Sara, who had met Smith and brought him home to show Sam during a mob trial she had covered years ago, ascribed his phenomenal courtroom success to juries unable to squelch a desire to take Smith home, feed him a decent meal, and give him a clean tie.

"Actually, I think we've got it under control." Sam set a plateful of eggs in front of Smith. "The cops were here Sunday night, we told them who we bought the chest from, and that pretty much puts an end to our involvement."

The doorbell rang.

"Bet that's the cops," Smith said, raising a forkful.

It was the cops.

Or, more precisely, one sour-faced cop with nude-colored legs, accompanied by a harassed lackey with a baby face and wrinkled uniform.

"Why, Sergeant Graber, what a lovely surprise," Sara said.

"I have some bad news for you," Graber said. She smiled. "It seems that the owner of Farm Salvage, a Mr. Marlin Bainey, has never heard of you. He didn't remember ever seeing you."

"That's absurd, Graber," said Sara. "How did he sell us a chest on Sunday?"

"You tell me," Graber said. "His store was closed Sunday. So I guess we'll have to take it from the top again, won't we?"

"We told you. We drove to Pennsylvania. We ate lunch. We—"

"Sara, shut up," Smith said. He stepped in front of her and said smoothly, "Sergeant Graber, I'm Stanley Smith, of Hargrove, Feldman, and Mercer. Are my clients under arrest?"

"No, of course not. I'd just like to ask them a few more quest—"

"I'm sorry, but under the circumstances I'll have to ad-

vise my clients very strongly against making any statements."
Smith shot a warning look at Sam and Sara. "If you have any
questions, you can address them to me."

"Well, there's the matter of Mr. Calvesi. I was hoping we
could clear this up amicably," Graber said.

"I bet you were," Sara muttered.

"You were saying you questioned this store owner, this
Mr. Bainey, and he said what?" Smith voiced Sam's unspoken
question.

"The local police in Lancaster spoke with him yesterday.
They even showed him photos—"

"What photos? We didn't give you any photos," Sam
said.

"Your driver's licenses."

"*Ayacck,* those hideous things? You sent our driver's
license pictures to someone to be used as a means of identification? That's libelous, that's inhuman. Smith, I direct you to
draw up court papers, I want the New York City Police sued
for defamation of character. Name her personally," Sara
pointed at Graber.

"This is not a joking matter," Graber said.

"No, it's not," Smith agreed. "And again, I'm sorry, but
I'm afraid that's all we have to say until I've had a chance to
consult with my clients further," Smith said. "Here's my card,
Sergeant. Give me a call anytime."

After the door had closed, Sam said, "What the hell was
that all about? Never seen us? Never sold us the chest? The
guy's obviously lying."

"Obviously, but until the cops have a chance to figure
that out on their own, I don't want you two talking to them.
At all," Smith said.

"Oh, come on, we can't be in trouble. We didn't do
anything wrong. This is America," Sara said.

"Smith may be right." Sam was worried. "Let's forget

this whole mess and worry about getting our newsletter done. We have to go back to Lancaster to review a restaurant anyway."

"Forget Lancaster. I want you two to stay out of Pennsylvania until this thing is settled," Smith said. "Until the police figure out where the guy was killed, we won't know who has jurisdiction over this case. And with the Pennsylvania cops launching their own investigation, I don't want you bumbling around there."

"But we can't stay out of Pennsylvania, Stanley," Sara said. "We have a deadline. We have to review the Shady Maple smorgasbord. We have to get the eastern Pennsylvania issue written in two weeks."

"Sara, Sam, look at me," Smith said. Suddenly the blue suit seemed almost to fit him. "Stay out of Pennsylvania."

That night, while Sam was reading in bed, engrossed in an essay on fly fishing, Sara paged restlessly through *Vogue.*

"Quit it," said Sam.

"Quit what?"

"Kicking me."

"I'm not kicking you."

"Then call the police."

"Why?" Sara asked.

"Because somebody just kicked me. And you're the only one who's authorized to be in this bed."

Sara groaned, tossed *Vogue* across the room, and tucked her head into her husband's armpit. She flung her arm across his chest. She said, in a voice muffled by chest hair, "It's just so weird."

"Two midgets in one lifetime?"

"Two midgets in three months."

"Yeah," Sam said. "It's weird enough to buy a pine chest that contains the butchered body of a dwarf. But it's almost statistically impossible to also have another midget—a midget hit man, yet—with a vendetta against you. I mean, it makes sense that the police would believe we killed Calvesi."

"Sam, maybe we should have told the cops about Martinez."

Jim Martinez had become a good source of theirs while they were reporting a series on the inadequate training given to state prison guards before they were sent into the cellblocks. Martinez had spent ten years patrolling the second tier at Sing Sing before deflecting a jagged shank with his forearm. The experience had made him amenable to detailing the dangers of prison life encountered by the people who carry the keys.

"We're the guys everybody loves to hate," Martinez had told them when they met him at the Elmira Correctional Facility, where he had been transferred following the knifing. He was now a union rep and helped steer young felons to the appropriate prison programs, matching the insane with psychiatric wards and the educable with high school extension classes.

"Nobody understands how hard it is to be a guard. We're not exactly sympathetic figures, but hey, we didn't put these guys in here." He jerked his head toward the honeycomb of steel bars that lined both sides of the claustrophobic corridor.

Martinez had liked the series, which documented the unsafe working conditions that guards endured, and had remained a helpful source over the years. The time Sam wanted to talk to the Freeway Sniper, who was doing life, Martinez passed along a note and arranged a telephone interview.

Three months ago Martinez had done them another favor.

"I hope I'm not overreacting," he said. The three of them were drinking coffee from a canteen truck parked at a gas station across from the Brooklyn House of Detention. Martinez had driven down to transport a load of state-ready prisoners. Cars whizzed by on Atlantic Avenue. They huddled under the Sabrett's hot dog umbrella to keep the icy raindrops out of their coffee.

"What's up?" said Sara.

"I heard something I thought you should know. It's your buddy Calvesi."

"How is the little fellow?"

"He's a little nuts," Martinez said. "And he's no fan of yours. Parole board says he's getting out pretty soon. The word is you're the first people he wants to see."

"What do you mean?" Sam asked.

"Pal of mine works at Sing Sing, knows I talk to you guys. He says Calvesi hasn't forgotten why he's there. He subscribes to your newsletter."

"That's nice," Sara said.

"Yeah. But he doesn't read it. He wipes his ass with it, pardon my French."

Sara mouthed a silent "Oh."

"We don't have anything hard on the guy, I mean, he hasn't said he's going to do anything specific, it's just that, you know, I thought you guys should know."

But it hadn't really been something they had wanted to know, since after all, there was nothing they could do to keep Calvesi in jail. It was just a nagging worry, at least that's all it had been for months.

"Do you think the body is Calvesi?" Sara asked. She lifted her head out from under Sam's arm to look at him. "I wish it was Calvesi."

"No way. That would be better than a Penn and Teller trick. We randomly go into a store in Pennsylvania, pick out a chest, bring it home, and poof, there's Calvesi?"

"That's why it's so weird," Sara said.

"That's why you kicked me?"

"I didn't kick you."

Sam yawned theatrically and draped his arm around his wife. He pulled her against him and sniffed her hair.

"Watch it," she said.

"Be glad to," he said.

She sat up, and, in a move that Sam believed that only women could do, crossed her arms and whipped off her sweatshirt.

SEVEN

Half a mile before Sam even realized they were approaching the Easton bridge, Sara started rooting in her purse for two quarters.

"Need fifty cents," he said as the iron girders came into sight.

He glanced over, saw Sara's outstretched palm.

"Thank you, Jeeves."

The coins clanged into the automatic toll machine, and the gate rose as tantalizingly as a stripper's skirt to unveil the industrial landscape of Easton.

"Welcome to Pennsylvania," Sara said in her best tour guide voice. "Birthplace of the Philadelphia cheese steak, Hershey's Kisses, Unique Pretzel Splits—and one tiny, misplaced corpse. And not a flake of snow in sight. So it looks like we're going to be about five hours early for dinner."

"Let's go shopping," Sam said.

"You, shop?"

"I want to get a glass-fronted bookcase," he said.

"You wouldn't, by any chance, be thinking that we should see if there are any nice bookcases at Farm Salvage, would you?" Sara asked.

"How did you guess?" Sam asked. "While we're there, I'd like to ask that Squidly guy—what did Graber say his name was? Bainey?—to explain why he lied to the cops about our being there on Sunday."

"Sam, I thought you didn't want to get involved. It's not our murder to solve, you said. We're not cops, we're food critics, you said. Et cetera, you said."

"It's gnawing at me. Either this guy Bainey lied, for whatever reason, maybe because he's the murderer, or else the Lancaster cops screwed up and showed him the wrong pictures or something."

"That's a more plausible scenario. Cops are cops, after all. And these were cops sent on a mission by the Graber monster."

"We drive near his place anyway, right?"

"Okay," Sara said. "Even if we don't get answers, we might pick up a bargain. We are hurting for bookcases."

An hour later they reached the Lancaster Valley, where snow-covered humps of earth were spread like a heavy comforter across an unmade bed. In the summer the pastures formed a green-and-brown checked pattern; now, only tiny houses dotted white wrinkles.

Once upon a time, Sara told Baby, a glacier moved sedately across this land, leaving smooth rolls behind to mark its course. "Can you say 'alluvial plain'?" she asked Baby. "Alluuuvial."

"Is that true?" Sam asked.

"I have no idea."

"Maybe we should try to get her to master Da-Da first." They passed Leininger's Wagon Repair and pulled into the dirt track beside Farm Salvage. Baby, droopy as a bunch of old celery in the car seat, let out a wail when Sam braked in front of the barn.

"You love this store," Sara reminded her as she lifted the infant from the car. "This is where Mommy and Daddy bought the dead body to give to the ugly police officer." Reassured, Baby stuck one sticky fist into her mouth and twisted the other into Sara's hair.

The barn had only nominally become a shop by virtue of the shelves of dusty colored-glass bottles and long tables of rusted axes and wooden planers marked YOUR PICK: $5. Inside the unheated building, Sam and Sara could see, far above, the wooden rafters that framed the barn. Under the corrugated tin ceiling the rafters spoked out from a sturdy center beam, a clue to historians that the barn was probably less than 140 years old. Long linen runners were draped across the rafters to catch pigeon droppings, which otherwise might have stained the brown-edged paperback copies of *Serpico, The Stepford Wives,* and *Jaws* that a customer could buy for 25 cents apiece.

Judging by the rich odor of manure and animals that permeated the shop, the barn had housed livestock for most of its decades. Even now, in the cold of January, a few tenacious flies buzzed around the merchandise.

Despite the cold, the barn seemed cheerier today than it had seemed on Sunday, Sam thought. Better lit. And from a back corner a radio was playing, tuned to a local weather and news station. From the vicinity of the radio a cheery voice called, "Be right with you."

The man who emerged from the back was short and fat, and broken blood vessels made his cheeks look like the inside of a pomegranate. His yellow rubber boots came up to his knees.

"Can I help you?" he asked.

"Just browsing," Sara said.

"Browse away." He smiled and wandered off to tinker with the space heater, a big gray box of a thing that was wheezing warmish air into the barn.

Sam called after him: "Do I smell pig?"

The man stopped and turned around to face him. "Pig it is. We raise them. Butcher 'em too. In the market for a freezer pack?"

"Might be."

"Pigs? I love pigs," Sara said. "Baby want to see piggy?"

"Want to see a pig?" the man said to Baby. Baby squirmed expectantly. "Cute kid. Come on out back. All the pigs you want."

The man led them out a back door and onto a shoveled walk that led to a field surrounded by a barbed wire fence. "This your store? Great place," said Sara.

"Uh-huh," said the man. "Been raising pigs for, oh, five years now. Good supplement to the salvage business. Been doing that for twenty-five years."

At the far end of the field was a shack, about the size of a large doghouse. The man pulled the strands of barbed wire apart and slipped through the opening. He grabbed a stout stick from the frozen ground and walked over to the shack. "Come on out, Scarlett you great big sow!" he bellowed, pounding on the metal roof. "Scarlett, you fat pig!"

With his thick Pennsylvania Dutch accent, it sounded like "you fate peeg."

"I loved *Gone With the Wind*. Ever seen it? Great movie. I had a hog once. Named him Rhett. We can't very well name a female Rhett, so we call her Scarlett. I always liked that name." The man continued pounding on the metal roof. "I

46

swear, you cannot raise a pig from a nap in the dead of winter." He pounded harder. Soon a great snuffling could be heard. It quickly escalated to a stentorian snorting. And then a pink, porcine snout, wet and bristly, protruded from the doorway. Hot vapor puffed from its nostrils.

Then the beast emerged.

Scarlett was big as a Japanese import, but all front end, like an American car. She was white with large black patches and small red eyes. Her tiny feet seemed inappropriate, like high heels on a circus fat lady.

"There she is," said the man. "Her father was state champion." He patted her hammy flanks affectionately, and Scarlett nuzzled his pocket, looking either for food or a pat on the head.

"Are you going to eat her?" asked Sam.

"Naw. She's too old and tough. Just use her for breeding."

Baby looked at the pig and smiled the broad smile adults usually reserve for best friends. Scarlett looked at her suspiciously, then started rooting. She sucked up a small clump of frozen rocks and dirt.

"Pigs'll eat just about anything, I swear," the man said. "You know, you don't look anything like those pictures the cops brought in." He stared at Sara, then at Sam, and his bright blue eyes narrowed. "The pictures the police brought in the other day were of you two, weren't they?"

"Yeah," Sam said. "That's why we wanted to talk to the man who was working here Sunday and sold us the chest. We're looking for Marlin Bainey."

"You've been talking to him. That's me."

"Oh, then they must have gotten the name wrong. Who was working here on Sunday?"

"Look, I don't want any trouble, especially from the police," Bainey said. He started back toward the barn.

"We don't want any trouble, either," Sam called after him. "We just want to talk to the guy who sold us the chest."

Bainey stopped. "I'll tell you what I told the troopers: Nobody was working here Sunday. The store was closed. The store's never been open on Sunday, not for twenty-five years."

He walked back to lift aside the barbed wire while Sara climbed through with Baby.

"What about the chest, Mr. Bainey? Did they show you any pictures of the chest?" Sam asked.

"Buddy, a chest's a chest. Except in New York, where people will pay an arm and a leg for anything. Uh, no pun intended. That's why I ship them there as fast as I can get them. Now, if you folks will excuse me, I got some work to do inside."

Sara started to cry.

Bainey paused.

Baby started to cry.

Bainey let his arms drop. Then he turned toward them again. Sucker, thought Sara.

"Come on, now, don't cry." He held his finger out to Baby.

Baby grinned a big, toothy grin and grasped his finger. "Babaga," she said.

"She said Bainey, did you hear that? Her first word," Sara said. Baby sniffed. "We don't mean to make trouble; we're just really confused and we want to clear this up—for the baby's sake."

"Cute kid," Bainey observed. They walked back to the barn in silence.

"Sir, we really were here on Sunday and we really did buy a chest here," Sara said. "It was sitting right over there by the door, and there was a box of buttons on the floor right next to it; Baby was playing with them."

"Yeah, there's a box of buttons, but I don't remember a chest. And I don't remember you. And the store was locked up."

Sam, standing near the buttons, idly picked through the

box. "Hey, what about this hook? Where'd it come from?" he asked.

"Oh, that." Bainey shrugged. "You see a lot of them around here. The Amish use them to keep their vests and coats closed. They figure buttons are too fancy, so they use hooks and eyes."

"The dwarf was Amish?" Sara asked Sam.

"Maybe," Sam said.

"Hey, why are you asking questions, anyway?" Bainey said. "Seems like you'd want to stay out of it."

"Well, when you find somebody dead in a chest in your living room, it makes you kind of curious," Sam said. "Makes you wonder who he was."

"The Amish hate curious," Bainey said. "They don't mingle with the English—that's their word for anybody who's not Amish—and they don't much care to answer English questions."

He thought for a moment.

"There is one guy who knows everyone around here. Name of Fisher, Dr. Jake Fisher. He's some kind of researcher out of U. Penn. I read about him in the *Inquirer*. Expert on the Amish, knows 'em all for this study he's doing. Maybe he could help you."

"Do you know where he lives?" Sam said.

"Naw, he doesn't run in the same circles I do," Bainey said. "Guess he isn't much interested in pigs."

"Thanks anyway," Sam said, taking out his wallet.

"Buddy, I don't think I told you anything worth paying for."

"Since when do you give your freezer packs away for free?" Sam asked.

"For you, I'll throw in a couple of extra hooves," Bainey said.

"Good for soup," Sara whispered to Baby.

EIGHT

The morgue's whining electric saw had split the rib cage and robbed the rubbery gray body of whatever measure of dignity remained to a cadaver with no hands, no feet, no head.

The assistant medical examiner was dictating into a microphone that dangled from the white-tiled ceiling. The tiled room produced a slight echo. "Cause of death, cardiac arrest. Subject exhibiting advanced stages of arteriosclerotic heart disease. Valve ruptured after occlusion of coronary artery." He sounded bored.

Stavropoulos sat on a stool two feet from the subject. He was eating a sandwich. He was scribbling notes. He interrupted the recitation. "So, Mikey, who do you like in the playoffs? I got a lot riding on the Jets."

The white-coated pathologist glanced over at him. "Stefan, you're dripping ketchup on the clean floor. Will you watch it?"

He clicked on the tape recorder. "Further tests will be necessary to determine whether cardiac arrest was precipitated or accompanied by damage to missing appendages," he droned on. "Unusually high levels of epinephrine detected in the subject's bloodstream."

"Epinephrine? That's adrenaline, right?" Stavropoulos said. He put down his sandwich on the edge of the autopsy table and flipped to a new page in his notebook. "Scared to death, huh?"

The assistant medical examiner nodded. "Jets by three," he said.

Stavropoulos considered. "Risky," he said.

"They looked good last week," the pathologist said.

"*Nyahh,* I mean the dwarf. Risky cutting him up like that. You figure so much blood must leave a trail a mile wide," Stavropoulos said.

"There really wasn't much blood, probably just a little bit more than the amount of ketchup you've dribbled all over the floor," the assistant medical examiner said. "The appendages were severed postmortem—you can see there's little or no swelling along the edges of the wounds—and so the flow of blood was greatly decreased."

"Can I ask you a question? You ever think about a book?"

"What book?"

"Writing a book. Wildest cases. Famous Corpses I Have Known. You know, inside the autopsy room stuff. You get a ghost writer. You could make a lot of money on the side," Stavropoulos said.

The assistant medical examiner looked up from the stomach he had sliced open with a very sharp scalpel. "You know," he said, "there was The Pisser. He was a good one."

The Pisser had been a homeless man, unfortunate in that the MTA had padlocked the dilapidated men's room in the subway station where he had taken up temporary residence. In his haste to answer nature's call from the edge of the subway platform, the man had accidentally sent a stream of urine sizzling onto one of the electric rails. The current traveled along the liquid, resulting in burns and charring that would not soon be forgotten even among the most callous of those who wield the knives in the city's morgue.

"Yeah, but there's no real mystery there," Stavropoulos said. "You need murder to sell a book in this town."

"Well, this is my first dwarf," the assistant medical examiner said. "And he appears to be a homicide. We know the generalities of the case already; now it's up to you and that Attila the Hun partner of yours to come up with some specifics."

Stavropoulos crumpled his ketchup-stained sandwich bag and meandered off to type up his notes—which ended up, a mere three hours later, in one of the two manila files that sat in front of Graber, their edges exactly parallel to the edges of her battered metal desk.

She flipped through the report in the file on the left.

Reading through the summary of preliminary autopsy results, Graber imagined the midget hanging by his feet from a rafter somewhere, his heart exploding as he watched Sam's menacing approach, a growling mini chain saw in hand, as his witchy wife danced a tarantella. The image would be terrifying enough to give anyone a heart attack.

Much of the report was inconsequential. Blood type A positive, like millions of other people in New York City. Ate his last meal about an hour before he died. Stomach contents still being analyzed. Body had been cut up by something sharp.

"Something sharp," Graber muttered disgustedly. That

was too sloppy even for Stavropoulos. She would mention it in a memo.

She picked up the phone, dialed Stavropoulos's home number, and said, "Something sharp? Detective, didn't the medical examiner's office narrow it down any further?"

Stavropoulos, used to these calls, said, "Hi, Evvie. Working late again?"

"Evvie?" Unprofessional. She would mention it in a memo.

Stavropoulos sighed, the long and loud sigh he saved for these calls. "Yeah, yeah, he did say something about the cuts looking like they were made with a cleaver thing or something. You see the picture of the wounds? They measured and decided the hilt of a cleaver must have made those dovetailed edges."

"A cleaver? Hacked with a butcher knife, perhaps? An implement found in any well-stocked kitchen? Interesting," Graber said. She hung up.

Graber sipped from a Styrofoam cup half full of tepid black coffee. It was bitter. She took another sip. The buff-colored file on the right side of her desk was labeled "Calvesi, Dominic." Graber opened it, scanned it for the third time in an hour, and flipped it closed.

She cleared her throat, dialed again, and said sweetly into the phone, "Lieutenant? Detective Sergeant Graber here. I'd like to talk to you about the body in the chest—"

"Goddammit, Graber! Who the hell gave the press that cockamamy Calvesi story?"

"I have no idea."

"Like hell."

"Harry, we really need to talk about this."

"Get your ass in here. I only have a few minutes."

Walking through the fluorescence of the hallway, the re-creped soles of her Earth shoes squeaking on the scuffed gray linoleum, Graber rehearsed. Lieutenant, my findings lead me to believe there's more to this than . . . no, too oblique. Lieutenant, a careful analysis of these two cases indicates . . . no, too dry. Damn, she thought, I should've put it in a memo.

Erbatz was late for dinner. Graber never went home for dinner. "Okay, Graber, make it fast," he said.

"The autopsy report shows the corpse was in his mid-fifties. Calvesi's fifty-three," Graber said. Erbatz sighed, but she pressed on. "The red-brown body hair is roughly the same color as Calvesi's. Unfortunately, we have none of Calvesi's hair for confirmation. The blood types match. Again, we don't have a sample of Calvesi's blood to cross-check the genetic markers."

"You still think this is Calvesi? Two galloping gourmets banging the hit man of one of the most violent crime families on the East Coast?"

"Well, they have a good reason to want him dead. His Sicilian reflexes would hardly have been dulled in jail. And we know from informants upstate that he held them entirely responsible for his jail sentence. If we know it, they knew it. You're not talking about Mr. and Mrs. John Q. Citizen. You're talking about two people who have sources every bit as good as ours."

"You're suggesting they launched a preemptive strike?"

"A dead dwarf we can't identify turns up in a chest in their apartment. They say they bought this chest in Pennsylvania. But the store owner says they were never there."

"I read the report, Graber. The clothes on the corpse are indicative of those worn by Amish farmers in eastern Pennsylvania."

"They're not stupid people, Harry. Rude, maybe, but not dumb. Who knows where and when they acquired the clothes? Who knows where and when they might have killed Calvesi?

One other thing. The ME's office says the murderer or murderers may have used a meat cleaver to hack him. They're cooks."

"Give me a break. According to the report, the postmortem dismemberment was accomplished very neatly. With a very sharp knife. None of the jagged hacking you see on drug dealers. Indicates someone who knew what he was doing. A surgeon, maybe. A cook, no."

Erbatz went over to his aquarium and flicked a fingerful of food into the water. An angel fish sailed to the surface.

He went on. "The angle of the cuts indicates a left-handed person chopped him up."

"The husband's left-handed."

"All right, Graber, let's assume they wanted to kill him. Wouldn't it be easier just to dump him on the street, where we'd think his buddies got to him?"

"Maybe, Harry. But life isn't always so tidy. These are very clever people. People used to manipulating facts."

"Keep digging, Graber." Erbatz frowned.

"Yes, sir."

"When will we have results on the fibers?"

"Tomorrow."

"Keep me updated."

"You got it."

He nodded. They both stood up. Erbatz went home.

Graber went back to her desk and finished her cup of coffee, which was now quite cold. She liked it that way.

NINE

If the corpse's clothes were fastened with hooks and eyes instead of buttons, he must have been Amish, Sam thought, so—

"Think out loud, please."

They were in what once had been some farm family's front hall. But that had been years ago. Today there was no woven rug, no pile of ready firewood, no heavy woolen coats and caps hung on pegs beside the door. Instead, the chilly entryway was filled with three dozen people, packed together as tightly as the kernels on an ear of corn. Each person clutched a little slip of paper—an admission ticket to visit this Guaranteed Real Amish Farmhouse.

Sam and Sara were huddled over Baby, who lay on a bench in the corner of the hall, in the throes of exchanging a used disposable diaper for a new one. A voice crackled over a loudspeaker: "Five minutes until commencement of the tour. All children are asked to remain silent for the duration of the tour."

Sam looked over his shoulder as a camera, belonging to a tourist, accidentally poked him in the right kidney. "I was just wondering why the driver of the car also has to change the infant," he said.

"Rules. You know the rules," Sara said. She scooped the diaper wipes, the Desitin ointment, the cornstarch, and the changing pad into the backpack that traveled everywhere with them. She zipped it shut.

"But if you had changed her in the car, while I drove, it would have saved time," Sam said.

"Rules. I don't make them. I just follow them," Sara said.

"Just once I'd like to meet the person who does make the rules around here."

"Can't. Rules. Besides, if you spent your time thinking about who the corpse might be—and don't say Dominic Calvesi—instead of trying to trick me into changing Baby's diapers—very nice diapers, don't cry, sweetie—we probably would have solved the murder and have been awarded a plaque from the PBA by now," Sara said. "We could use more plaques on the wall in the den."

"We don't have a den," Sam said. "And I still don't think this tourist trap is going to tell us anything useful about the Amish. What kind of historically authentic Amish farmhouse has a gift shop? Are we supposed to believe that Amish farmers routinely manufacture Keystone State ashtrays?"

"Skeptic. It's the best lead we have right now."

"Actually, I wouldn't mind getting a look at the books for this place. At five bucks a head, they must make a helluva lot off the tourists who come through here," Sam said. "Wonder where it goes."

"I know, I know: 'probably a money-laundering scheme.' You're regressing to your newspaper reporter days," Sara said. "Don't think fraud. Think murder."

"Sure, Frenchie."

She patted him on the butt as they joined the other tourists shuffling up a narrow staircase and into a cramped room. A bed and scarred chest of drawers indicated that real people had once slept where tourists now tromped.

"Questions after I'm through in each room," a tour guide, who looked as if she had been drawn by James Thurber, announced in a loud and nasal tone. She strode through the crowd to stand by the headboard, shuffling her note cards. "Please, no talking. If children can't keep quiet, please wait in the parking lot with them." She stared meaningfully at Baby.

Baby smiled.

The tour guide looked away.

She consulted her notes. She cleared her throat and read from an index card titled "Bedroom, Male."

"This - is - where - the - male - children - slept - all - in - one - room - and - they - hung - their - clothes - on - pegs - instead - of - in - closets - and - were - not - allowed - to - grow - facial - hair - until - they-married," she said in a single breath. Her glance raked the tourists, challenging them to ask questions. The tourists nervously fingered their camera straps. A four-year-old girl whimpered, but her mother quickly clamped a hand across her mouth and smiled weakly at the tour guide. A short man in the corner flipped through a guidebook.

"I have a question," Sara said.

"Yes?"

"Those shirts hanging on the wall. They have hooks, but no buttons. Why?" Sara said.

The tour guide shuffled her note cards, looking for the one titled "Modes of Dress, Male."

The short man in the corner looked up. "I think it's an

indication the people who owned those clothes were Old Order Amish, who believed in a strict code of plainness. It says that the hooks are still very common among the Old Order sects," he said. "Of course, who knows. I bought this guide-book in the gift shop."

A little boy by the window rolled his Mattel car on the sill. *"Vroom vroom,"* he said softly to himself.

"KEEP THAT CHILD QUIET, PLEASE," the tour guide barked. The group tensed. Sara clutched Baby protectively.

In the kitchen the guide pointed out the oil lamps, used because no electricity was allowed. "You'll notice," she said, "a lack of ornamentation. The linoleum that has been scrubbed so often that the pattern is worn off . . ."

"Ma," whispered the four-year-old.

The guide stopped talking. All eyes were on her. She glared at the four-year-old felon. The child looked at her feet. One minute elapsed, and then a second. The tourists' hearts pounded as one.

"The kitchen is really the center of the Amish home, where the family gathers not only for meals but also to read the Bible, to talk, and sometimes to relax before bedtime. That's why you often see a sofa—like that one—in the corner of the room. And you will notice some signs of hominess—the hand-embroidered hand towels hanging beneath that mirror, for instance. A prospective bride would make those and bring them to her new home after the wedding. They're purely orna-mental. In exchange, instead of a fancy diamond engagement ring, her fiancé would carve her a tall wooden clock, like the one you see next to the sofa."

The man with the book cleared his throat tentatively.

"Yes?" the guide snapped.

"How did the Amish get to Pennsylvania in the first place?"

The tour guide sighed, a sigh much like the exasperated noise a drill sergeant would make during Saturday inspection if confronted by a barracks full of recruits wearing unshined belt buckles. The tourists cringed collectively, mentally catapulted onto the set of *An Officer and a Gentleman.* Only the little boy, determinedly racing his Hot Wheels Corvette under the legs of the pine table, failed to react.

The guide shuffled, resignedly settling on a card labeled "Amish, Origins."

"In-the-1600s-when-William-Penn-learned-of-their-religious-persecution-in-Europe-he-invited-the-Amish-to-settle-in-Penn's-Woods-a-land-grant-from-the-king-of-England-that-today-is-known-as-Pennsylvania." Perhaps she was late for another appointment, Sam thought.

"A land grant from the King of England?" Sam asked. "Just some extra acreage the king had lying around, a whole state's worth of woods?"

The guide peered at him, then down at the little boy whose car was zipping around the toe of Sam's loafer.

"LITTLE BOY," she said, her face reddening, "IF YOU CANNOT BE QUIET YOU WILL HAVE TO WAIT OUTSIDE."

"I have a question," Sara said.

The guide looked at her.

"WHY ARE YOU SO MEAN TO CHILDREN, YOU OLD BAT?"

The tourists focused their attention on the guide's shocked face. This was an answer they all wanted to hear.

"Babababa," Baby gurgled happily, as she left the room on her mother's shoulder, headed for the lobby and a refund.

The secretary answered on the third ring: "Psychiatry department."

"Hello, this is Dr. Alma Bates calling from Des Moines for Dr. Fisher."

"I'm sorry, he's on sabbatical," the secretary said.

"Yes, I know, he's doing field work in Lancaster County. I have the data he wanted on gene pools in the Amana colonies. He did sound as if the information could be pertinent to his current project. Do you have a number where I could reach him?"

"Sorry," the secretary said. "We don't give out home numbers."

"I see. Do you have a mailing address for him, or would it be better for me to write to him in care of the department and explain that the information was delayed because I couldn't get in touch with him directly?"

"Well, I guess I could give you a mailing address," the secretary said. "Uh, let's see . . . Nine Corn Row Path, Ephrata. Zip is one seven five two two."

Sara wrote down the address, thanked the secretary, and skipped from the gas station's pay phone back to the car.

"Success," she said, tracing the route to Fisher's house on a map.

"You're pulling out all your old tricks today," Sam said. "First tears at the pig farm, then intimidation at the Fake Amish Farmhouse, now impersonating a scholar. The last time I saw you cry to get information, we won a Pulitzer."

Sara had, in fact, perfected her technique (more sniffs than sobs; why risk puffiness?) while assuming the identity of a novice restaurant owner. As the proprietor of Chez Guevera, she had on one teary occasion begged the deputy health commissioner's bagman not to close down the rat-infested Soho eatery while he was awaiting a payoff.

"Now that was crying in a good cause," Sam said.

"This is a good cause, too. It's clear that if Bainey got on the stand and swore he never saw us at his store on Sunday, he'd be telling the truth. And it's equally clear that we're never going to learn anything relevant to this case by touring a tourist trap," Sara said. "So we've got to move forward. Unless you want Baby to visit us behind bars for the next twenty years? Besides, practice is good. I'm feeling rusty."

Sam looked at her. "You miss it, don't you?"

"Don't you?" Sara asked. "Don't you feel a little twinge when you hear the whiny voice of Max Goldberg on our answering machine, that snively timbred sound that used to control our lives?"

"No," Sam said. "I much prefer him begging us to come back to ordering us to cover some two-bit politician's press conference. What do you miss most—the long hours, the low pay, or working for people who became editors because they didn't know how to be good reporters?"

"I know, I know," Sara said. She hoped he wouldn't bring up the copy editor incident in front of Baby.

"What about the time you tried to run over a copy editor because he changed your lead?" Sam said. "He could've pressed charges."

"He changed the word 'people' to 'persons.' 'Persons in New York City.' I was a laughingstock."

"You miss that, huh?"

"No, Sam, what I miss is—"

"Is feeling like your job contributes to society?" he asked. "What's more important than eating? What makes persons happier? You should feel good because you're helping persons learn how to find good food and be happy. And you're working for yourself."

"You're right. I wonder where that copy editor lives now."

"Sara."

TEN

The green-shuttered stone house was distinguishable from its neighbors only by a laundry line, bedecked with frozen sheets and socks, that stretched from the porch to a bare tree in the backyard.

"I guess Dr. Fisher really likes that fresh-air smell on his linen," Sara said.

"He must use an ice pick to make the bed," Sam said.

Baby wailed demandingly. "Have we ever forgotten you?" Sara asked, lifting her out of the car. "Don't count that time at Balducci's."

A good minute after Sam rang the bell, the door swung open. The woman standing behind it was eating a bowl full of what could possibly have been library paste and pencil shavings.

The woman pushed her glasses back up onto her nose and squinted.

"Hello, we're looking for Dr. Fisher," Sam said.

"Me," the woman said.

"Dr. Jake Fisher?"

"No, Molly. My husband is Jacob," she called behind her. "What do you want with him?"

"Well, actually, we bought a dead body on Sunday—"

"She means we found it in the chest when we got home."

"But the store owner doesn't know any Amish so he said come here—"

"She means we hope Dr. Fisher can help us identify the dwarf."

"Jacob, you'd better come out here," Molly called. "Now."

Jake Fisher, wearing a blue work shirt (smells good even from here, Sara thought), came in from the kitchen, eating a bowl of paste and shavings.

"Cute kid," he said, and smiled at Baby. Then he looked at Sam and Sara and frowned slightly, a university professor cornered by two grossly overeager undergrads. "Yes?" he said.

"Dr. Fisher, my name is Sara Amstel, and this is my husband, Sam Popkin. A few days ago, while shopping for antiques"—at this last word Fisher began to glare irritably—"we bought a large, and we thought ideal chest. We bought it at a place called Farm Salvage? Over on Route 30?" Fisher did not respond. "Anyway, we bought the chest, got a good deal on it, and loaded it into the back of our car. . . ."

"Ms. Amstel did you say your name was?"

"Sara."

"Sara, I do not mean to be rude, really I don't. However, unless I finish putting down on paper all the brilliant observations I've made today, I will not be able to file on time the

64

pithy and, I might add, compelling grant application sitting on yonder table."

He gestured with a jerk of his thumb toward the dining room behind him, and the computer that sat atop the table. "And if I fail to file on time that pithy and compelling grant application, I will lose funding for my research. And if that happens, dear lady, I will be back at the University of Pennsylvania, wiping the noses of engaging though intellectually undeveloped freshmen as they slog their way through Bio 101."

Sam cut in. "We're sorry to bother you, Dr. Fisher. But Sara and I were hoping you could possibly help us identify a body."

"A body?"

"A body we believe belongs to an Amish person," said Sara. "A body that we found when we unlocked the chest that I was just telling you about."

"Goodness," said the other Dr. Fisher. "How awful."

"Why are you trying to identify this body? Isn't that a matter best handled by the police?" asked Jake.

"Doctors Fisher," said Sam, "we live in New York City. There is at least one homicide a day in New York City. The police have their hands full trying to keep up with the paperwork on the violent deaths of the natives. We're afraid that this murder—obviously the killing of a Pennsylvanian—will receive little if any notice. We feel a personal commitment to at least try to identify the victim." Sara gave Sam a look that the Doctors Fisher, had they seen, would not have noticed, but which Sam understood as: I love the way you lie.

Jake Fisher sighed and gestured his three guests inside, toward low, comfortable chairs he had recently reupholstered in his garage, and offered yogurt and granola (one mystery solved). He settled himself onto the orange shag rug that undoubtedly came with the undoubtedly rented house.

The room was furnished as if by accident, filled with the

detritus of an academic's life. Books, papers, a U. Penn coffee mug littered the room. Bright hex signs painted on a wooden board hung over the fireplace. A series of bleak black-and-white photos of Amish boys walking into a barn were hung over the brown corduroy convertible sofa.

"Aside from purchasing this chest in the heart of Amish country, what makes you think your victim was Amish?" Jake asked.

"He was wearing dark clothes with hooks instead of buttons, suspenders—well, a broken pair, that is—and . . ."

"A hat?"

"Uh, well, not exactly. The dead man's head, hands, and feet were cut off," said Sam.

"Goodness," said Molly Fisher. "Someone doesn't want this person identified."

"He was a dwarf," Sara said. "That's what the medical examiner said."

While he listened, Jake Fisher frowned, reached behind him for a pipe from a three-tiered rack of briars, filled it gently with Rattrays #6, and lit it. From time to time he punctuated the story with a nod.

"I really do think this is a matter for the police," Molly said.

She was obviously not a woman who concerned herself with fashion trends; she was wearing a butterscotch-colored A-line skirt constructed of some nubby polyester and topped by a lime dacron blouse with dolman sleeves. Her shoes were wedgies. She fidgeted nervously with her ankle strap.

Her husband ignored her. "Dwarf," he said.

They waited while he took a puff and blew smoke rings into the air.

"Did you know that dwarfism is unusually common among the Amish?" Jake said.

They did not.

"In fact, somewhere in my papers I have a couple of studies that were done, years ago, looking at the occurrence of dwarfism among the Lancaster Amish. I seem to remember there were two different manifestations. The Amish society is so closed, so inbred, that, statistically speaking, its members are really much more at the mercy of recurring genetic defects than the rest of us. Dwarfism just happens to be one of the more common defects around these parts."

"So the fact that he was a dwarf definitely supports our theory that the corpse was Amish?"

"Certainly," Jake said. "It also might make it easier to identify him. Which just reinforces my feeling that it would be a wild goose chase to ask around."

"Why?" Sam asked.

"How much do you know about the Amish?"

"Well, we've seen *Witness,*" Sam said.

"Twice," Sara said.

"Hmmm," Jake said.

"Harrison Ford aside, that movie didn't have much to offer," Molly said. "Better give them the short version, Jake."

"Short version?" Sam asked.

"Long version takes a whole lifetime," Molly explained. "Jake was raised Old Order Amish, in Mifflin County, west of here. So he knows enough about it."

"Molly, please."

Sara lit up. "Dr. Fisher, I knew you could help us. How fascinating—please go on. How did you end up a university professor?"

Jake smiled crookedly and blew out a thick spurt of smoke. "My mistake. Not that I thought it was a mistake when I was a youngster, of course, before I became acquainted with the ugly intricacies of departmental politics and the thicket of intrigue that surrounds one's attempts to get tenure at a large, bureaucratically moribund institution. But I'm getting ahead of myself."

They waited through another couple of puffs.

"I guess you know that most orthodox Amish quit school after the eighth grade," he continued. "The feeling among the order is that too much education makes one less than humble, and humility, alas, has always been my weak suit. Anyway, I was too good in school to give it up. I liked it too damn much. When I was fourteen, the night my father told me I would not be going back to school anymore, I ran away, to Philadelphia. Got a job, moved into a boardinghouse, and enrolled in school."

"All by yourself? No help from your family?"

"To my family I was as good as dead. If I had been Jewish, like Molly, my parents would have sat shiva, like hers did when she married me. I wrote to them—uh, my parents, that is—to let them know I was alive and safe. But I never expected them to come looking for me, and they didn't. *Meidung* is the German word for it—the shunning. In the Old Order those who fall from the path are, in effect, excommunicated. Members of the family and fellow congregants are forbidden to mingle with the shunned member. But we're getting ahead of ourselves." He tamped his pipe lightly with his thumb and puffed.

"The first thing you need to know about the Amish is—my case aside—the high value they place on family. Families work the land together, worship together, live together with grandparents who have their own apartments, called *grossdaadis,* attached to the main house," Jake said. "Each family belongs to a different district, a group that worships together. Everyone in a given district knows everyone else's business. It's a deeply interlocking and closed society."

"Which means for your purposes," Molly said, "if anybody was missing, much less murdered, everyone would know about it. We might have even heard about it, and we haven't."

"We've been working here, off and on, for a couple of years, and we know just about everybody. I'll show you."

Jake led them into the dining room, or what could have been a dining room if the long pine table and its six chairs had not been piled high with dog-eared copies of medical journals, computer spreadsheets, and notepads covered with scrawled equations and doodles.

In the middle of the table sat the computer, its blinking cursor at the top of a screen full of grant application lingo. Jake sighed again, stored the application, and called up an intricate spiderweb of a chart.

"That's the family tree for one branch of the Lapp family—just the generations that are living now," Jake said. "We've been pretty painstaking about compiling this data because it's the foundation for the study we're working on: We're trying to establish a hereditary link to certain types of schizophrenia. The Amish are perfect for a controlled study, A, because they meticulously document their ancestry, and B, because they are such a small and isolated group."

"Kind of like Gilligan's Island?" asked Sam.

"Pardon?" said Jake.

Molly picked up the explanation. "What that means, for your purposes, is that everybody around here is related to everybody else in some way. So it would be kind of hard for anybody to disappear into thin air."

"Your work must be fascinating," Sara said reflexively.

"All in all, we'd rather be rich and retired and living in a crumbling castle along the banks of the Dordogne," Jake said. "But—"

Sam cut in. "I understand what you're saying about how close-knit the Amish community is. But we really do think there's a chance the body we found belonged to an elderly Amish man."

"Because of the clothes?"

"Right."

"Well, the clothes you described are very plain, probably Old Order Amish and not Mennonite. Mennonites are much less strict. They wear the same clothes you—" He looked at Sara's oversized man's tweed jacket, sleeves rolled up, black tights, and tiny black skirt. "The same clothes I would."

"So how would we find him?"

"There's really no centralized place to call or person to ask. It would mean a lot of hard work, a lot of asking around among the different districts. But luckily for you, I do a lot of field work. I'm going out tomorrow to interview some members of the Weavertown Amish. You can come along. They may not know anything, but you have to start somewhere."

ELEVEN

Baby and Penguin held fast to the sides of the shopping cart as it whipped down aisles of cutlery, glassware, and kitchen gadgets.

Zipppp past the microwave-safe baking dishes.

Whooosh around the stacks of remaindered cookbooks.

Waaaaaa as they made a sharp left turn and almost caromed into Sam, who was bent over a display of steamers.

"She looks like she's going to throw up," he observed.

"Nonsense," said Baby's chauffeur. "She lives for speed. She needs a little pair of goggles."

"Well, then, I might throw up. In disappointment," Sam said. "Frenchie—"

"No fish poacher?"

"No, and I've dreamed of cold poached snapper. Prepared in a sauce of Cabernet Sauvignon. And Chiou Chow Style. I guess this detour was a waste of time, after all."

"Don't fret, sweetie, we might be able to help you out." And they were off, cart *shruuushing* around the coffee makers and out of sight.

Sam straightened, looked around the cavernous expanse of the kitchen equipment factory outlet, and decided he would settle for a wire basket for grilling fish fillets.

But no sooner had he banished the hope of acquiring a severely discounted poacher than his family, slightly sweaty from nefarious exertion, reappeared at his side.

"Sara, where'd you find that poacher?" He gestured toward the box that covertly nestled in the bottom of the shopping cart, under a set of place mats and a wooden cutting board.

"Oh, I don't know. I guess a new shipment came in while you were over here," she said.

"Sara, you poached that from somebody else's cart."

"It looked like it was abandoned."

"Is this the sort of example we want to be setting for Baby?"

"Better petty thievery than rubbery fish."

They queued up at a cash-only register. The pilgrimage always ended too quickly. For weeks on end Sam would lie on the couch at home and scheme. What should he buy the next time they drove to the outlet? A Melitta one-cup coffee maker? A specialty blade for the food processor? Sam, never much for shopping, believed that if one had to make purchases, this store was the wise shopper's mecca.

It was housed in what looked like a big red-brick warehouse—in fact, it had been a textile mill until the early 1970s. Behind its parking lot lay West Reading, and beyond it the dirty Schuykill ("Is that a joke spelling?" Sara asked) River, and beyond that block after block of well-kept rowhouses that climbed halfway up Mount Penn.

"Maybe we should move to Reading," Sam said, loading up the car. "Good clean, country air. People are nice. Washers and dryers in the home. No people from New Jersey."

"Not again," Sara said. "Every time we leave Manhattan, you start talking about moving. Albuquerque. Montreal. Nashville, for God's sake."

"Yeah, but Reading is different. A good place to bring up kids. Lots of nice family neighborhoods where Baby can trike around. We could get a farmhouse. Live off the land."

"No seltzer delivery."

"And no traffic. And no kids bashing in car windows to steal radios."

"Sam, I know you can't help having this nostalgia for small towns. It's your Midwestern upbringing. But if you really, truly, honestly think we should move out of the city, then I think the only place to consider is Arizona. Next door to your parents. That way, at least, we get ready-made babysitters."

Sam's parents, a seemingly ordinary couple who had raised three children in a perfectly nice suburb of Chicago, had one quirk. They no longer could stand civilization.

The misanthropy overtook them slowly. At first they had appeared to be like any other couple on the verge of retirement. They sold their house and moved west, to Colorado. But after a few years they started complaining about too many busloads of skiers. They moved to Butte, Montana, where the land was wild and the neighbors sparse. After a few years they started complaining that the dog down the road was sniffing around their bushes. They moved to a ranch on the outskirts of Boise. But after a few years they started getting junk mail.

Now they lived in an adobe house, high on a mountain about twenty miles south of Kingman, Arizona. Their closest neighbor was a telephone pole down the rocky dirt road. Their only intruder was TV. The nearest traffic signal was a fifteen-minute drive. To get their unlisted phone number, Sam had resorted to calling a friend who worked for Southwestern Bell.

"Move near my parents? Sara, the only way to get close to their place is to parachute in from a helicopter. It's easier to drop in on Howard Hughes than my parents."

"They have a weakness. Grandchildren."

"But I have a weakness. I need conversation. At least once a week."

"I'm glad you see it my way. If our building goes co-op, we'll buy."

Sam started the car. Dusk was falling. Behind them, at the top of Mount Penn, a Chinese pavilion whose tiered roof—outlined in red neon at night—was visible from most neighborhoods of a city proud to be famous for its factory seconds.

No one seemed to know why the Pagoda was there.

"I still don't get it," Sara said, getting into the car.

"What, the Pagoda?"

"No, Farm Salvage."

"You mean Bainey saying we couldn't have bought the chest from him? It is puzzling," Sam agreed, cutting in front of a tour bus. A banner on the front of the bus said, BARGAIN HUNTERS FROM THE BUCKEYE STATE.

Baby started crying. Her mother reached behind her, freed the infant from the torture car seat, and plopped Baby into her lap. "There's nothing wrong with people from Ohio," Sara said, soothing the shrieking child. "Your father went to college there."

"Iowa."

"Whatever."

"As near as I can figure it, we're right and Bainey is right," Sam said.

"Go on."

"Well, here's what we know logically: We were there. We bought a chest. We took it home," he said. "And here's what Bainey knows: The store was closed. He never saw us before. He doesn't remember the chest."

"If he's telling the truth. So what follows?"

"What follows is that somebody else—our friend the human squid—must have broken into the store for some reason on Sunday. We must have surprised him. So he pretended to be the store owner to get rid of us."

"But, Sam, Bainey would have noticed a break-in. Jimmied lock. Shattered window. Something."

"Maybe the doors weren't locked. Or maybe the guy had a key."

"And came in through the barn doors? And forgot to close them behind him?" She wasn't convinced.

"Sara, you got out of the car first. Before you got to the door, you yelled back at me. You said it looked open. What made it look open?"

"I saw two men among the merchandise, over by where the chest was. Wait a minute, I must have seen them leaning over the chest. Sam, did I see Squidly stuffing a body into the chest?"

"Okay, so they're doing something. Then they go into the back room to do something else or to get something. Squidly hears us in the store. He comes out to get rid of us."

"And we say we want to buy the chest. Sam, he smiled when we said that. He perked right up. We got rid of the body for him."

"I guess that would make him the murderer. But why haul the body to the store? Did he kill him in the store? If so, there'd be evidence—blood, bone, gore."

"And Bainey would have told the cops. Unless, of course,

Bainey had something to do with the murder, which I don't believe. So where does that leave us?"

Sam sneaked a glance in the rearview mirror and saw Baby slumped in the car seat. "That leaves us with a sleeping third wheel," he said.

"A deeply sleeping third wheel," said Sara. Her finger traced the corduroy grooves that covered his leg. "I'm feeling kind of sleepy myself."

Sam yawned elaborately and steered the car toward the hotel.

TWELVE

Edward liked to think he was good at crossword puzzles. Or, more precisely, he wanted the tenants who passed his desk in the lobby to think he was good. He did not understand most of the clues, so he filled in the blanks more or less randomly, trying to alternate consonants with vowels. He always used ink.

"Hmmm, six-letter word for 'incompetent,' " Edward muttered. He chewed on the tip of his pen and tried to look "ruminative," a clue in yesterday's puzzle that he had looked up in the dictionary.

Words like "ruminative" and "congers" were not words he would have learned at public school in Queens. Or at least they weren't words he had learned before dropping out of the eleventh grade when his father, a super at a good building in the East Seventies, got him his first job as a floorman in this Upper West apartment building. He worked the janitor's job for two years before being promoted to doorman. He hoped to be superintendent within a few years. If not here, somewhere better.

That was the beauty of the profession. You never knew where it would take you. You never knew what excitement would come walking in your door each day. Take Sunday night, for instance, when the (strange-acting) folks in 9P asked him (suspiciously, he now realized) to help them lug that (odd-looking) chest up to their (eerily clean) apartment.

Of course, now that he thought about it, Edward had noticed a few things that might be of interest to the authorities.

The lobby's revolving door spun. Edward chomped on his pen, stogie-like, and mumbled absentmindedly, "Ditzy . . . six-letter word . . ."

"Nitwit," said 4B, coming through the revolving door. In one hand she held a leash attached to a straining rat terrier. In the other she balanced four gift-wrapped packages. One fell to the floor.

"Perfect. Thanks," Edward said, filling in the letters and making no effort to help. She disappeared into the elevator. Pen poised to fill in the blanks with a flourish, he waited for someone else to enter the lobby.

That someone, unfortunately, paid little attention to the doorman's labors. He was a short—some might say dwarfish—man with a bad haircut. If Edward had been a vice cop, he might have recognized the ragged work of a prison barber. The man wore a messenger's uniform, pants neatly creased.

With a glance Edward appraised the situation: (1) The fellow, clearly a menial, had no TP (tip potential), and (2) He is smaller than me. Faster than a computer with a 486 chip,

Edward decided his own course of action. I will ignore him, he thought. Let the rascal see who's king of this lobby.

The messenger scanned the tenants' directory under the glass top of Edward's desk. He worked a wad of gum between strong jaws, jaws as muscled as the rest of his hard body.

"Hey, fat boy." The words fell like a gavel. Normally, Edward would not have allowed such impertinence to pass. But something in the messenger's voice and stance persuaded the doorman to overlook the hostility—for the sake of amity between the classes.

"Excuse me?"

"I got a letter here for delivery to Sam Popkin and Sara Amstel."

"I'll sign for it."

"No. Got to be hand-delivered. In person."

Edward shrugged, gave a cold grin. "They're not here." He turned back to his crossword puzzle.

A muscled hand slapped down onto Edward's newspaper, ripping out the puzzle page.

"Hey!" Edward was startled. Where was a man safe if not in his own lobby?

"Sorry," the messenger said. "First day on the job. I'm a little nervous." He smoothed out the page.

Edward looked into eyes that made him wish he kept a doberman behind the desk. "Uh, maybe you want to go up and check, anyway?" he said. "9P."

The messenger nodded his thanks.

Up on the ninth floor the messenger wasted no time ringing the buzzer or knocking. Instead, he pulled a series of lock picks from inside his jacket pocket. After a few seconds of manipulations inside the keyhole, the messenger heard the satisfying sound of the dead bolt pulling back. He went inside.

What a pigsty, he thought, surveying the premises. But no

surprise. Never did an honest day of work in their lives, so no reason to think they'd bother to dust the baseboards.

The man stooped, ran one gloved finger over the coffee table, and shuddered. Where to start? He nervously fingered his gold ID bracelet.

In the bedroom a long wall was covered with framed photos. Black-and-white. Head shots, mostly, of the brat. Baby with teeth. Baby with no teeth. Baby drooling. Baby waving a rattle.

In the corner was an easel. Half-finished canvases were stacked against it. Looked like someone was in the middle of painting a fright scene. A horrific, beady-eyed face surrounded by lanky strands of hair was half-finished. One eye already had been painted a hellish red.

Suddenly the apartment seemed too cold, musty, a little empty. Not in here, the man thought. Too easy to miss.

The kitchen might be better. Filthy in here too, though, he noted, as his heel crunched a stray Cheerio. Randomly he pulled open cabinets. What the fuck is Basmati rice? He'd been here long enough, he thought, reflectively rubbing the raised letters on his bracelet.

The bathroom was cluttered with tub toys. He squeaked a rubber octopus. He noticed the new issue of *Consumer Reports,* with an article on radar detectors, next to the toilet. He was tempted.

Five minutes later, the elevator door opened into the lobby. King Edward, still on his throne, was still working the ACROSS boxes. His Majesty looked up nervously.

"You were right, not there," the messenger said.

"Took you quite a while to figure that out," Edward said.

"Did it, Fat Boy?" The same disproportionately large, though neatly manicured, hand came down and grabbed the puzzle page. The messenger spit his gum into the paper and neatly folded it up. He gently stuffed the balled-up waste into Edward's shirt pocket.

"When do you expect them?" the messenger asked.

"I don't know, I don't know," Edward said. "They've been gone since yesterday, and they took the car. I think they're out of town."

The messenger chucked Edward under the chin. He winked and said, "I'll be back."

College graduates frame their diplomas. Or tack the tassels from their mortarboards onto bulletin boards above their desks. Or subscribe to alumni magazines. Very few, however, are nostalgic enough to hoard the yellow highlighting pens they used to mark textbooks while cramming for finals.

Even fewer use those yellow felt tips to highlight passages in three-page memos sent to their bosses years later.

Evelyn Graber, Fordham '81, had a file cabinet full of highlighting pens. She used them to mark the carbon copies of the chronologically filed memos that filled the other two beige (almost nude-colored; a coincidence?) metal cabinets that stood in her living room, sentries on either side of a nice deep window that other people might have framed with bookcases. Or stereo speakers. Or chairs.

But other people—wasters of time who listened to music and read novels and slouched in overstuffed chairs when they could have been at work boning up on advanced forensic techniques—would not have been promoted so quickly through the highly competitive ranks of the New York City Police Department. Other people would not have compiled such an impressive homicide arrest record that they were considered sergeant material at age twenty-eight. Other people would not have researched affirmative-action hiring policies thoroughly enough to exude an odor of "Promote this woman or she'll sue your ass off."

Other people would not write so many memos.

"Pithy," Lt. Harry Erbatz said, nervously flipping through the neatly typed memo.

Words like "deep-fried dough," "confectioners' sugar" and "digestive disintegration" leaped out at him.

"You'll notice, Lieutenant, that the contents of the victim's stomach indicate he had eaten about two ounces of a sweetened pastry," Graber summarized. "The properties and ingredients of the pastry are indicative of a deep-fried Italian dessert called bomboloni. From the extent to which the victim's gastrointestinal juices had processed the food, it appears he ate within an hour of death."

Erbatz was beginning to wish he had skipped his morning Danish.

"Very complete," he said, scanning the bomboloni recipe, key ingredients highlighted, that Graber had affixed to the last page.

"So, Lieutenant, while the ethnic nature of the stomach contents is not conclusive by itself, it supports the theory that the victim could be Calvesi."

"I see. What about the final autopsy results?"

"A few important findings here, sir. First, we know the victim was a dwarf; that's obvious from the size of the torso and the limbs. The type of dwarfism—extremely rare, actually—is known as the Ellis-van Creveld syndrome. If we could see his hands we'd probably see polydactyly—"

"Huh?"

"Six fingers. That really defines the abnormality. Likewise, if we had his head, we'd probably see bad teeth."

"Well, we don't have his head or his hands."

"True. But the type of malformation of the chest cavity is what frosted it for the ME. The respiratory system was really out of whack. He was quite certain that this corpse was that of an Ellis-van Creveld victim."

"Great. Do Calvesi's medical records from prison indicate that he suffered from this deformity?"

"They indicate he had a lot of colds—respiratory malfunctions, clearly—but no X-rays were taken of his chest. And no one seems to have ever taken exact measurements of his chest or limbs. As for his hands—well, no one has ever said he has six fingers. Something like that would have stuck out. He probably had the extra digits removed."

"What about the fiber results?"

"Inconclusive," Graber said. "No follicle or color match between the victim's hair and samples found elsewhere in the apartment. However, we did isolate dozens of red wool fibers on the victim's clothes, which may indicate what the murderer was wearing."

"The struggle is beginning to sound like a real brawl. There should be physical evidence at the scene."

"We can't rule it out. In any case, if either suspect has a red wool shirt that matches, we would have strong circumstantial evidence."

"Either suspect?"

Graber colored. "I'd like to bring them in for more questioning, Lieutenant."

"You don't need my permission to question witnesses, Graber."

"They have not been cooperative," Graber said. "And they aren't at home."

"Before we assume that the 'suspects' fled the jurisdiction, perhaps you should call their lawyer. And let me know when you hear from the FBI crime lab on the origin of the fabrics."

Three minutes later, back at her desk, Graber was listening as Smith stonewalled. Smoothly. He didn't learn that silky tone at Fordham Law School, she thought, flipping through an open copy of Martindale and Hubbell, looking for his name.

"I don't understand how we can help you, Sergeant," Smith said.

"I have a few more questions."

"Why don't you tell me what they are and I'll try to get you the answers."

"I'd rather ask them directly," Graber said, her finger running down the page in the lawyers' directory on which were listed all the employees of Hargrove, Feldman, and Mercer. It was a long list.

"I'll have to confer with my clients. I don't know what their schedule is."

"You are in touch with them, I hope?" She found his name and overlined the entry with a yellow felt tip: Smith, Stanley, graduated Harvard Law in 1978, clerked for a federal appeals judge, served a stint in the U.S. attorney's office, now in private practice. And makes about $250,000 a year, she thought. Silky-toned bastard.

"Sergeant, my dealings with my clients, as you are well aware, is of no concern to you."

He doesn't know where they are, either, she thought.

"Mr. Smith, this is not that difficult. I must speak with your clients. If you cannot produce them, I will bring them here myself."

"Are you planning to arrest them?"

"I hope that's not necessary," she said.

"Not only is it unnecessary, it's absurd. You don't have probable cause."

"Some judges might consider it probable cause to arrest two people who had a motive to kill a gangster whose body turns up in their apartment."

"Gangster? You mean you have a positive identification on this body?"

"Mr. Smith, you know I can't discuss details of an ongoing investigation with you. Look, this isn't that difficult. I want to see your clients. I want to see them at one P.M. today. Will you produce them or do I get an ADA and a warrant for their arrest?"

"Impossible."

"You mean you don't know where they are?"

He ignored the question. "I have to be in court this afternoon."

"Tomorrow then. Noon." She hung up.

Smith hung up, a beat late. Behind him enough empty cans of Diet Coke were stacked on the windowsill to form a pyramid that partially blocked his view of the Statue of Liberty. A rumpled and somewhat stained white shirt, still wearing a tie, was draped over the leather chair by the door. Tall stacks of depositions, court transcripts, and probation reports littered the floor around the deep mahogany desk where Smith sat, doodling on a legal pad.

He buzzed his secretary.

She came in, navigated around the slippery piles of documents, and wordlessly set a can of Diet Coke on his desk next to a humidor half full of Te-Amo Meditations. She did not comment on the picture Smith was drawing of a muscled leopard ripping apart a bird, feline fangs dripping blood onto feathers scattered across the legal pad.

She closed the door very softly behind her.

Smith took a cold, caffeinated, dietetic swig and, without turning, poured a generous amount into the pot of a waxy green philodendron on the windowsill. Cigar butts poked up like tombstones in the soil near its roots. Generally suspicious of greenery, Smith had become particularly wary of his firm's rented houseplants after bumping into a tall and prickly cactus by the receptionist's desk. Three weeks ago, when he had discovered one green tendril wrapped around the leg of his chair, he had vowed to kill this philodendron.

The plant was thriving.

Smith swallowed more Diet Coke. He sketched in nude-colored panty hose on the leopard. Then he drew a long green tendril around its front paws.

As a lawyer, he was unruffled. Either his clients would turn up or they wouldn't. In any case, it was doubtful they had anything to do with the murder (although one thing the practice of criminal law had taught him was that, given the right circumstances, anyone was capable of doing anything). Even if they were arrested, it would be little trouble to get them out of jail.

But as a friend, Smith was worried. He knew, from the moment he had advised against the trip, that Sam and Sara were headed back to Pennsylvania. And he knew, from his previous life as a prosecutor who had dodged their dogged questions with repeated "no comments," that they would be looking for answers.

They're perfectly rational clients who are cognizant of the consequences of their actions, the lawyer thought. They're nosy snoops who don't know when to mind their own business, the friend thought. I haven't even been formally retained in this case, the lawyer thought. I should be watching out for them better, the friend thought.

Shut up and start earning your six thousand dollars a week, the lawyer told the friend. Turn your attention to a paying client—that bail-reduction application to be filed in the case of an earnest businessman who owned a fleet of trucks and had, inexplicably, been charged with harassing a competitor with a chain saw.

Instead, the friend picked up the phone and dialed Sam and Sara's answering machine to leave another in a series of increasingly acerbic messages.

THIRTEEN

The twin yellow stripes that run down the middle of the New Holland Pike are there for a good reason. The twisty two-lane road is far too narrow to allow a driver to pass another car. And barely wide enough to maneuver around a horse-drawn buggy, whose orange reflective triangle is a meager concession to the twentieth century.

In the summer, when the Amish farmers head to market with corn and pole beans in their boxy black buggies, the tourists back up for miles, a snake of cars waiting to strike the next Real Penna Dutch Diner or Amish Farm Village that appears over the rise. And whenever a driver wants to make a left turn into the gravel lot of the one-room schoolhouse where tourists' pamphlets are handed out, the snake behind stops slithering. For a moment.

But in the winter wet cotton-colored snow, turned even grayer in the late afternoon twilight, coated the trees and houses and buggy paths that sloped away, down the valley on either side of the pike. Jake Fisher's defroster was on high to offset the hot air inside the car, most of which was emanating from his mouth. The windshield was still so foggy that he almost missed the turnoff near Blue Ball.

"While this strip of Lancaster County is most famous to New York tourists who want to buy overpriced quilts, it has very little to do with the way the Amish live," Fisher said.

They passed a covered Amish buggy, its spoked wheels rolling along at a decorous ten miles per hour.

How slowly the day passes in the company of a bore, Sam thought. A bore who drones on and on about his work and how important it is and how important he is and—

"See that?" Jake motioned as they passed the bearded farmer holding the reins. "What does that tell you?"

"A buggy? That the driver's Amish," Sara said.

Jake let her answer hang in the air.

"Probably?" she said. "Maybe?"

"Probably. More than likely," Jake said. "Some orthodox Mennonites favor buggies as well. But the careful observer would see much more than just the buggy. Did you know, for instance, that the buggies different Amish groups drive are as distinctive as the tribal attire of American Indians? Some buggies have gray tops. Some black. Some groups' buggies have buckles. Some don't. Different groups use different horses to pull their buggies."

Of course we know that by now, you droning old bore, Sam thought. We've been talking about little else since daybreak, when we started this godforsaken scavenger hunt for a corpse. By suppertime we're going to be ready for a pop quiz on local customs.

Already, they had visited half a dozen farmhouses scattered across the Lancaster Valley. They had breakfasted on scrapple and shoofly pie with the Mook family. They had eaten homemade ham-salad sandwiches with the Zooks. They had watched while Jacob Esker milked his cows. But none of the Amish farm families they visited knew of a dwarf who was missing, or of anybody else who was missing, for that matter. Sam was ready to call it a day.

"Some of the differences in custom between one group of Amish and another are very, very slight—to an outsider," Jake said. "But to the Amish the differences appear great. Not just in buggies. But the hats they wear. Their clothes. What they eat. Their rules for acceptable behavior."

"You mean one group might split from another just because they don't want to wear the same hats?" Sara loved to play good student. In college she had always arrived at class five minutes early, sat in the front row, and nodded thoughtfully whenever the professor made a particularly good point.

The droning showed no indications of abatement. "They split for a lot of different reasons, your example being oversimplified, but the right idea. You have to remember that the Amish, and I use that term as a general umbrella to describe dozens of sects," (Oh brother, Sam thought, slumping sulkily in his seat. He speaks in footnotes.) "were a splinter group to begin with, Lutherans who split with the church because—and I'm simplifying again, of course—they didn't believe in baptizing babies who were too young to understand the ramifications of joining the church," Jake said.

"And they just kept splintering?" Sara really could be insufferably perky.

"To this day," Jake said. "There are dozens of different sects in Pennsylvania alone."

Wait a minute, Sam thought.

"Wait a minute," Sam said, sitting up. "This could be useful. You mean that if the corpse we found had some unique characteristic—some tribal marking, so to speak—we'd be able to narrow down where to look for him. We wouldn't have to go around talking to all these different groups, right?"

"Right," Jake said.

Sara was excited. "Well, what about the hooks and eyes on his clothes?"

"Common to most Old Order Amish," Jake said.

"Old Order?" Sam asked.

"They're the strictest groups. Don't usually allow cars, electricity, mingling with outsiders."

"Like this Weavertown family we're going to see?" Sara asked.

"Actually, no, the Weavertowns split with the Old Order. They're more like the Beachy Amish, who generally allow those modern conveniences and even are using English instead of German in religious services. But there's no telling. Your corpse could be a Weavertown who wears Old Order clothes, for all I know. It's possible."

Jake guided the car off the narrow road, onto a rutted dirt path that sliced through two flat fields. The frozen gray earth gave no hint of the crops that would be sown there in another three months. The dirt track dipped and climbed, and as the car edged over a gentle rise Sam and Sara saw a boxy white house about two hundred yards ahead.

Here comes Dead End Number Seven, Sam thought.

"Remember—you're graduate students. Assistants," Jake said, parking the car on the edge of the narrow driveway behind the kitchen door. "The husband is in the barn, the wife is probably cooking inside, and the children aren't home yet from school. I think this will be our last stop today."

"Oh, no, so soon." Sam tried to sound casual.

Sara shot him a look as they walked up the back steps.

Mrs. Brower met them at the open kitchen door. "Professor Fisher, how are you?" she asked, wiping her hands on the very clean white apron she wore over her brown ankle-length dress. "I've been watching for you."

They stepped inside, into the cleanest kitchen Sam and Sara had ever entered, with a floor so painstakingly waxed that Baby probably would slide across the length of it and slam into the far wall if she ever tried to crawl on the white linoleum. Rachel Brower smiled.

"These are two of my . . . assistants," Jake said. "Sam Popkin and Sara Amstel. They came along because they've never met any real Amish people before."

"Pleased to meet you," Rachel said, knotting her apron nervously in her fists. "I'm heating up some peppermint tea, if you'd like."

"That would be delightful," said Jake. "Sure is cold out there."

Sara swept the room with a glance, contrasting the reasonably high-tech, well-appointed kitchen with Rachel's crudely cut dress, with its unhemmed cuffs and its neckline fastened with straight pins instead of buttons.

Rachel poured boiling water from a teakettle into a steel pitcher that had been lined with dried peppermint stalks. She let the tea steep, then decanted some into four mugs that she had lined up on the long, scrubbed table that ran down the middle of the kitchen.

"I drew up a list of all my cousins and their cousins, like you asked, Professor Fisher," Rachel said, smoothing a sheet of lined paper on the table in front of Jake. "And I think I can tell you where most of them live."

"Good, good," Jake said. He pulled a pair of eyeglasses from his shirt pocket and polished them with the napkin Rachel Brower had placed in front of him.

Sam caught Sara's eye, looked down at his wristwatch pointedly, and yawned elaborately.

"Know of any midgets who might be missing, Mrs. Brower?" Sara blurted.

Rachel Brower, bemused, sat down hard.

"Uh, what my assistant means," Jake said, putting on the glasses and frowning at Sara, "is that we heard news from another family that the police in the county are trying to locate a dwarf—probably Old Order Amish—who was reported missing."

Rachel Brower turned red but said nothing. The back door swung open and in strode Rachel's husband, John. "God be with you," he said. He nodded at Jake and the visitors and carefully removed his heavy denim jacket and rubber boots. Then he headed to the kitchen sink and began scrubbing his hands.

"John, did you hear?" Rachel asked. "Someone has been reported missing to the police."

"Oh? And who is that?"

Jake said, "Actually, the police don't know who it is. They're searching for a dwarf."

"Oh?" John asked again. He stopped for a moment, then patted some warm water into the fringe of his Abe Lincoln beard. "A dwarf? There are a few in these parts. What does this one look like?"

Sam, who had been nursing his tea (was it possible this was his eighth cup today?), said, "Actually, Mr. Brower, now that I think about it, he looked kind of like you."

Sara looked sharply at her husband. What was he talking about? John Brower was a good six feet tall. And had both his hands and feet, as well as his head, intact.

John Brower smiled and dried his hands. "Must be a pretty tall dwarf," he said.

"Well, I don't mean exactly that he looked like you, more that he dressed like you," Sam said. "You're wearing pants held up with one suspender. The first time I saw this man—the only time, really—he was wearing heavy black pants, just like you, and I thought one of his suspenders must be broken. But now I realize that's just the style."

"One suspender!" Jake interjected. "A single suspender! Why didn't you tell me that he was a one-suspender?"

"What would you be seeking this man for?" John Brower asked Jake. He gazed seriously at the professor.

"I'm sorry, Rachel and John," Jake said quickly. "It's a second study I'm working on . . . missing people . . . or something . . . anyway, I think we'll have to cut this visit short today. I'll come back next week and we'll talk about your cousins and the genetic markers I think I've isolated in your family."

The Browers, frowning, nodded.

"By the way, Mr. Brower," said Sam on his way out, "you don't know of any missing dwarfs in your district, do you?"

"I can't say that I do," John Brower said.

"John," said his wife.

"Enough, Rachel. I'll walk these people out to the car."

Sam and Sara looked at each other, then smiled weakly at Rachel Brower and followed her husband out the door. Single file and in silence, they walked down the neatly shoveled path that led from the house to the driveway. Night had fallen, and so had the temperature. Jake and Sara got into the front seat and Sam in the back. They all looked expectantly at John Brower, who said nothing. He helped Jake shut the door. As Jake turned the key in the ignition, however, Brower tapped on the car window.

"The man that you're looking for, I believe, is named Emil Stoltzfus," he said. "The church don't have anything to do with him anymore."

He turned and trudged heavily away.

FOURTEEN

Lots of bitter coffee had been drunk during the past three hours. Lots of reports had been underlined in yellow. Lots of homicide detectives had been summoned and reprimanded for real or perceived errors.

As the clock announced the arrival of noon, Graber's phone rang. Shrilly.

"Yes?" she snapped.

"Sergeant Graber, good afternoon." Smith's voice would have soothed a baby to sleep.

"Mr. Smith, where are you? And where are your clients?" Graber asked, unconsciously mimicking the ring of her phone.

"I'm glad I caught you. I wanted to bring you up-to-date," Smith said.

"Mr. Smith, I thought we were up-to-date. We have an

appointment. For one minute ago." Dammit, she thought. I expected that organ grinder and his untrained monkey to show. Now what?

"Oh, dear, there must have been a misunderstanding. I was under the impression you wanted me to call you at noon today," Smith said. "How unfortunate. In any event, I've been in touch with my clients, and I think we may be able to arrange a mutually convenient time to meet."

"Mutually convenient? I want them in my office. Now." Think. Is there enough to justify arresting them? Graber wished, for once, to buy time. Let Erbatz decide. Let him be responsible.

"There's no problem having them come to your office. Oh, can I put you on hold for a moment? Thanks." Without waiting for a reply, Smith pressed the hold button. He loved to do that during negotiations. He picked up a letter opener from his desk and menaced the philodendron as the light on the phone blinked angrily. Suddenly the plant twitched. He quickly picked up the phone.

"Oh, I'm terribly sorry, Sergeant, where were we?"

"You." Graber stopped and took a deep breath. She was so angry that her knees were shaking. "You were about to tell me why I shouldn't obtain a warrant for their arrest and haul them in here for questioning."

"Please, Sergeant, let's try to behave like professionals." This was almost as good as torturing the plant. "We want to stress our eagerness to cooperate with the investigation in any way possible. My clients are understandably anxious to have this incident resolved as soon as possible, certainly before the police department becomes involved in a slander and defamation suit."

"Mr. Smith, I repeat, where are your clients?"

"Sergeant, I repeat, we're eager to cooperate. We can be in your office at ten A.M. Monday, if that's convenient."

"Monday? Monday is certainly not convenient. I need to speak with them today."

"I'm afraid that's impossible. We have unalterable scheduling conflicts."

"They've left the state, haven't they?"

"Sergeant, you know I would be breaching client–attorney confidentiality if I were to discuss any aspect of my conversation with them with you."

"I see. I think, Mr. Smith, that I'll need to confer with Lieutenant Erbatz about what steps we should take to ensure the speedy continuance of this investigation. The department is most anxious to question your clients immediately."

"Well, Sergeant, when you reach a conclusion, you know where to reach me."

He hung up, much cheered. So much for your bluff, he thought. Take that. He jabbed his letter opener in the air, careful not to point it toward the lurking green fronds. A more satisfying conversation, certainly, than the one with Sam an hour ago.

After hearing what he had been sure was an edited version of Sam and Sara's adventures, Smith had been shaken enough to swig from an old, fizzless can of Diet Coke.

"Let me get this straight. You harassed Bainey in his store. You lied to a secretary at U. Penn. You dragged a perfectly respectable professor into this mess. You refuse to return to Manhattan to cooperate with the police. And you have not yet paid my retainer."

"Smith, none of your histrionics, please."

"And now you're telling me you're going out to some Amish farms to ask the locals if any of their relatives have been chopped up into soup bones? Keep a diary, this could be a TV movie. 'The Sam and Sara Story: Two New York Nuts Invade a Peaceful Countryside.' "

"Smith."

"Sam. Sam, this is not like you. Sara I understand. She is amoral. She is unable to differentiate between right and wrong, a sociopath, really. You, however, are an adult. Why don't you get in the car, point it east, and once I figure you've crossed the Jersey line, I'll call the Graber monster and suggest she get the Lancaster County police to ask around among the Amish."

"We don't know for sure yet. We'll call you tomorrow," Sam had said. "Try not to worry. We'll be fine."

We'll be fine. Smith scowled. Fined is more like it. Fined and fingerprinted and locked away. Baby in little infant manacles, growing up on C Block with Sesame Street characters tattooed on her arms. Lying on a hard prison cot and smoking cigarettes while other little girls learned to color and paste.

Smith buzzed his secretary.

She came in, stepped over his raincoat and around an overturned chair, and, wordless, set a fresh Diet Coke on his much doodled-on desk blotter.

He considered asking her to tie a ribbon around the philodendron and to send it, via bicycle messenger, up to the police precinct. Instead, he poured it a fizzy shot.

If there were worse motels in the world, Calvesi did not want to know about them. The place gave him the creeps. Wormy cigarette burns crawled across the nightstand. A pubic hair curled up in the soap dish. The fluorescent tubes that lit the room fluttered and buzzed, about to die.

It was still better than prison.

Dominic Calvesi unpacked an overnight case, taking out his own sheets and remaking the bed. He rolled the grayish motel-issue sheets into a ball and stuffed it under the bed. From his bag he took out a linen carpet runner and smoothed it flat on the floor to stretch a bridge of cleanliness from the door to the bed. He took off his shoes and socks and sat them on a chair where he could keep an eye on them.

He lay, wearing only boxer shorts, on his clean white sheets. The bareness of the room was relieved only by his wallet, stuffed with new identification papers, on the low dresser, and a wad of chewed gum, rolled into a neat ball in the ashtray on the nightstand.

And a by now wrinkled messenger's uniform, size extra small, hung in a closet near the bathroom. He'd iron in the morning.

He would have to stand on a chair to reach the ironing board. He hated to iron. In fact, he hated to do many things that other people took for granted. He needed specially fitted hand pedals to drive a car. He needed stacked heels on his shoes so he could reach up to hand a quarter to a sales clerk behind a counter. He needed to stand on a chair to turn off a ceiling fan.

But he did not need any special equipment to kill people. A .357 shot from a Smith & Wesson Bulldog would pound just as hard into a man's chest or skull if the trigger was pulled by a very short person.

The man flipped through *New York Newsday*. He preferred the way the *Times* handled the news, but he couldn't stand to handle the Times: too inky. After glancing at his horoscope ("Good day to make friends"), he turned to the story he was looking for, "Food Critics' Tale Half Baked":

> Police are suspicious of the alibi of two former prize-winning investigative reporters who claimed to have found the dismembered corpse of a man in their Upper West Side apartment Sunday night, *New York Newsday* has learned.

Had they skipped town? the man wondered doubtfully. Had they really done the job on somebody? The guy I don't see killing anyone, except by accident with anchovy paste. But the wife. Her I'd watch. She could talk him into it. Maybe together, with her all earnest and sincere, and him, sneaking up behind somebody in his topsiders with a butcher knife. They knifed me in the back.

The article continued:

Police confirmed that they are attempting to locate Dominic "The Muscle" Calvesi, recently released from prison after serving a term for extortion, a crime that came to light in newspaper stories written by the former reporters.

Police said they were unable to rule out Calvesi as the murder victim.

The wiry hit man earned his mob moniker "The Muscle" when he cracked open the head of a rival by sandwiching it between his powerful bicep and forearm during an Ozone Park brawl in the 1960s, federal agents said.

What bullshit, Calvesi thought. If that had been the case, I'd be called the Nutcracker. In reality, he had been tagged with the name "The Mussel" in high school after eating nearly a bushel of them in a restaurant in Little Italy, where he had accidentally ordered a Bolognese dish called "cozze e patate," which he found surprisingly edible. He had continued to reorder the dish until the restaurant had run out of mussels.

The Muscle. Maybe I should write a letter to the editor, he thought.

Maybe I should kill the editor.

Calvesi daydreamed about the different ways to kill an editor. In his daydreams he was always quite tall. I could sneak up behind him, while he was writing headlines, put a .44 Magnum loaded with mercury-tipped slugs to his head, and splatter his brains all over the page proofs. I could intercept him on his way to a morning news conference and throttle him. That's mussel, m-u-s-s-e-l, I would say, watching his eyes pop and his pants darken. I love when that happens.

Homicide, Calvesi's vocation, was the one aspect of his life into which fastidiousness did not intrude.

Stranger than fiction. The cops think I'm dead and they killed me.

And here I am, hiding out in a Fort Lee motel, laying low until I can relocate. Calvesi had no illusions about the fate of a man who had ratted on his former friends. If his former friends could find him.

These two food writers are really in *il brodo*. The trick at the apartment was a good start, but with some planning, how much more trouble could a supposedly dead hit man cause them?

A lot.

But where were they? Calvesi picked up the December issue of *The Thin Man,* which he had subscribed to in the penitentiary purely to fuel his urge for vengeance. He hated the breathless prose. But lately he had found himself waiting eagerly for the next issue, keeping a list of restaurants he wouldn't mind frequenting.

He noticed that the current issue recommended a Japanese restaurant near the George Washington Bridge that was known for its gyoza. He wrote down the address. As he got up from the bed, his eyes fixed on a boldface box at the bottom of the back page: NEXT ISSUE: DUTCH TREATS—THE FOODS OF EASTERN PENNSYLVANIA.

The Muscle, er, Mussel, smiled.

FIFTEEN

"One suspender," Jake was muttering as he inched the car down the icy road. "Why didn't you tell me before? Could have saved a lot of time."

"I just thought of it now," Sam said. "The body was all curled up and cut up. I thought his suspender was snapped in a fight. It wasn't until I saw John Brower's flannel pants—"

"One suspender, plus hooks and eyes, equals the Bremmer district. The Bremmers are a small, unusually isolated sect. Most of them live north of here. I was very lucky to have made contact with the Browers. I hope you haven't ruined them as subjects for my study."

"He's a Bremmer, too?" Sara asked. "The body is a Bremmer?"

"You're going to have to find out for yourselves." The

car had reached Jake's house. "Come on in," he said, disappearing at once into the recesses of his home. Sam and Sara followed. Before they had time to remove Baby's bulky snowsuit, Jake had returned with a directory: "Descendants and History of Christian Fisher Family."

"This, my dear friends, is what makes the Amish an ideal group for geneticists to study. Their documentation of their bloodlines is even more comprehensive than the Mormons'. And this book is the most complete listing of every Amish person alive today. In fact, it lists a lot of dead Amish people as well. It even lists Amish who married non-Amish."

He opened the book to the index, ran his finger down a list of Stoltzfuses.

Sara looked over his shoulder. "Three Emil Stoltzfuses. Great."

"Don't despair. Only one lives within the area where the Bremmers are concentrated. Right here."

Sam wrote down the address. "Not far, just down the road," said Jake. "I've got a road map here someplace." He rummaged through the bottom drawer of an expensive-looking rolltop desk.

Baby began to squall. Sara looked at Sam, Sam looked at Sara. Baby looked at Sara, and redoubled her shrieks. Sam got up from the sofa and got a bottle from the small day pack that carried Baby's gear.

"Someone wants a nap," cooed the howling infant's mother. "Someone's verrrrry leeeeepy." Sam quickly prepared six ounces of formula and dropped the nipple into Baby's ready mouth.

"What are we going to do with her?" he asked.

"No problem," said Jake. "You can leave her here if you want. We could make up a place for her to sleep on the bed. I'm sure this won't take long."

* * *

The red flag was up. The mailbox looked like a rusted lunch kettle stuck on a post. Black block letters said it belonged to Emil Stoltzfus. And it was full.

Maybe Stoltzfus wasn't interested in the bills that bulged out the front of the white metal box. Or maybe he just hadn't felt like walking a quarter mile down his dirt driveway to pick up his mail.

Or maybe he hadn't been home in days.

The concrete house looked like a two-story cardboard box. A wash of black grime running down the side would have been more appropriate to a tenement between Avenues B and C than to a farmhouse off Elam Road, somewhere between East Earl and Gap. Past a stand of molting evergreens, Sam and Sara could see a silo, its rusted sheet-metal cone a harsh contrast to the green shingled roof (looks like somebody licked a thousand S&H stamps and pounded them on, Sara thought) on the house and the barn.

The house sat on a rise from which its owner could barely see the roof of the nearest farm, two miles away. It was hard, in the winter, to tell what Stoltzfus might have grown in the fields that were separated from the yard by a light-gauge mesh fence. Silage probably, sorghum and alfalfa to save money on feed for the cows lowing up in the barn.

Stoltzfus hadn't shoveled his driveway, either.

"Let's give it one more try," Sam said, looking up the driveway past a beatup pickup coated with snow.

"I don't think anybody's made fresh tracks since it snowed," Sara said.

This was their second visit to the Stoltzfus house, where they had arrived earlier and knocked on both the front and the kitchen doors. When no one answered, they decided to take a drive through the countryside to give Stoltzfus time to come back home, assuming he was not dead.

Now they stood in front of the house for the second time

in an hour. "This has been a stupid waste of time," Sara said.

"Most thorough reporting is," Sam said.

But, like all good newspaper reporters, they had been conditioned to complete any inane exercise in the pursuit of fact. It was reflexive: Follow any lead, no matter how seemingly irrelevant, make that extra phone call even if you already know what the person on the other end will say.

By collecting thousands and thousands of facts—most of which would never make it to print—the thorough reporter was able to repulse the idiotic queries of copy editors. (Once, Sam had written about a pack of rats that chased a jogger through Morningside Park. Question from the copy desk: "Norwegian Black rats or brown?") When the phone rang at midnight, the caller a copy editor who just wondered if anyone had asked if the murder suspect in a crime story had neat penmanship, the thorough reporter had the satisfaction of rattling off quotes from the suspect's third-grade teacher, now living in Boise. "Had trouble forming cursive letters, particularly *g,*" the reporter would say, "but I don't think we need to add that to the story. I ran it past the cops, and they didn't seem to think bad penmanship could be a motive."

"Oh," the copy editor would answer, nonplussed.

Reflexive habits die hard, which was why Sam and Sara found themselves for the second time stamping their cold, numb feet in the snow at the end of Stoltzfus's driveway.

"I wonder how long this mail has been sitting in here," Sara said.

"I wonder if it's a federal offense to just look in a mailbox," Sam said.

"I'm sure Stan would know," Sara said, opening the mailbox, pulling out a bundle of letters to examine the postmarked dates. "This stuff has been here for a few days."

"At least three days. Three newspapers," Sam said.

"It's not a crime to look through somebody's window, is it?" Sara asked.

Two minutes later, cloaked by an early dusk, Sara was sneaking around the back porch as Sam inspected the dairy barn a hundred yards away. The mournful lowing from within signaled impending starvation, Sam decided, as he walked past the stalls of emaciated cows. There were a dozen in all, so underfed that the outline of their rib cages jutted out under their slack flesh. "Poor guys," Sam said to the cows, as he opened the lids of the grain bins to confirm their emptiness. "No food."

At the back door Sara rattled the knob. "Anybody home? Hello?" she called in a too-loud voice. The knob turned. It was unlocked. She slowly pushed the door open. Inside, it was dark and not much warmer than the porch. Sara smelled gas as she stepped onto the linoleum floor of the kitchen.

"Pilot light out? Better not turn on the lights," Sam said, coming up behind her with a flashlight. He had once written about a man who killed his wife by filling the house with gas and unscrewing a lightbulb. When she flipped the switch later that day, the place blew like a *Miami Vice* drug dealer's Ferrari.

"Cows haven't been milked either," Sam said. "Or fed for a while. After we leave, we'll make an anonymous call to the Humane Society."

"The Humane Society feeds hungry cows?" Sara asked. She opened a window.

"Don't touch anything," Sam said.

"Mittens don't leave prints," Sara said.

"They leave fibers." He shined the flashlight over the counters, the pine farm table, a dilapidated couch in the corner. Someone had been here recently. But apparently not too recently—a frozen glass of milk sat on the table next to a half-eaten pretzel shape that Sam recognized as funnel cake.

The rest of the room was plain, in keeping with Amish custom, the only adornment a mirror, hung on the wall above a wooden rail that held an embroidered linen face towel.

For a simple, unadorned house, the place was pretty messy. Drawers and cabinets were ajar. Papers were scattered on the floors of the living room and kitchen, as if a window had been opened and a gale had blown through.

The front room was a little more orderly, filled with straight-backed chairs and an uncomfortable-looking settee. On the mantel were a Bible and some redware bowls. More redware was stacked on the floor under the front window.

"What a weird custom," Sara said. "Plates on the floor."

They walked over to inspect the plates. Sam trained the flashlight on the wood floor. The beam picked up a slightly burnished rectangular shape on the wood.

"Makes no sense," Sara said. "Why would you stain a dark spot on the floor before sitting plates on it?"

"You wouldn't. But if you put your plates on top of a nice big chest on the floor under the window, the sun would fade the wood around the edge of the chest," Sam said.

"Bingo," said Sara. "If you see any heads or hands lying around, keep it to yourself."

He didn't. Sam and Sara cautiously crept into each room of the house. But they found nothing more than what they already suspected—that Stoltzfus lived alone. And was missing.

SIXTEEN

Calvesi pumped the barbell past his occluding chest, then dropped his bent arms to his waist. He winced. Twenty-eight. He lowered the 100-pound freeweight, then pumped again, gritting his teeth. Twenty-nine. He was really sweating. Out of prison less than a week, and he already was getting out of shape. These curls were killing him. Turning him into an old man.

True, he was still in pretty good shape. Able to bench press his own weight a few dozen times without puking made him something of a small-person's Arnold Schwarzenegger, he figured. Central casting ever wanted to do an all-midget version of Hercules, they'd do well to find Dominic Calvesi.

He rolled off the exercise bench and wandered over to inspect the Universal. Better than the one we had in the joint.

Not as good as the weight room of the corner gym in the old neighborhood, where a group of aging, small-time fighters spent their afternoons punching a sweat-darkened bag. He had stepped up his workouts during his trial, at first to let off steam, later, when it became clear that he was headed for state time, for survival.

He strutted over to the bench press, set it for 180 pounds, and began pumping.

Calvesi missed the neighborhood. But not enough to go back there now. That would have been the first place they would have looked for him—Tony and Al and the old crowd he had done some free-lancing for. In order to keep his stay in the can down to a doable sentence, he had done some cooperating with the organized crime strike force. Nothing big time—he absolutely refused to testify at any trials. But he did tell them where to find the body of a renegade Long Island garbage carter who had been stealing stops from some of the others. Calvesi had expected to do the hit, but Tony went with some punk from Miami who offered to do it for ten large— half of what Calvesi charged.

Nothing was guaranteed anymore. Used to be you worked for a family as a full-time subcontractor. Any hit needed doing went to you. Not anymore. I wonder if it would be possible to organize a union of shooters. Not a bad idea.

Never one to let bygones be bygones, Calvesi had sent for the strike force boys shortly after arriving at the state prison, the day Calvesi's cellmate had used the little man's new toothbrush to floss his anal hair.

Calvesi told the state investigators only enough to get himself a private cell, as well as some time off his sentence. No big deal. On the other hand, Tony would probably have figured out that the cops hadn't just excavated under the south entrance of the Evergreen Office Park, in Deer Park, on a wild guess. Ground had been broken on the project—the project that was put together by Tony, Al, and some of their friends—about a week before the carter was hit. There weren't too many people who knew that, fewer still who would be willing to talk about it.

It would not have been a happy homecoming when they found him.

Of course, they wouldn't find him. Certainly not at a Jack Lalanne Health Spa in Fort Lee.

There was nothing wrong with this place, either, though the handgrips of the bench press were a little slick. Calvesi paused for a second and ran his hands through his Très Flores pomade-slicked hair, just enough to get his deformed fingers a little tacky. Then the man in the child-sized sweatpants and PF Flyer sneakers went back at it.

This place was the cleanest Jack LaLanne Health Spa he'd ever been to. Calvesi, a charter member whose unflagging patronage had proved very lucrative to the Jack LaLanne chain, slipped comfortably in and out of any of a dozen of the franchise's identical weight rooms. He liked the walls of mirrors, the bright lights, the smell of strong cleanser that overpowered the odor of sweat. Exercise always helped to clear Calvesi's head. And now, with a sinister but still vague scheme taking shape, he needed to concentrate.

Calvesi sat up, reached for his shockingly white towel—he always brought his own well-bleached terry cloths—and mopped his forehead. He was breathing heavily.

Getting a message to his father was out of the question under the circumstances. He still had a lot of work to do. There were many ways he could make life miserable for those pathetic food writers. He could kill them. He could maim them. He could maim their baby. These alternatives, the subject of long hours of daydreaming in his jail cell, remained viable. But why risk it, why put himself on the line, now that fate, for the first time in his life, had taken this beautiful turn? Calvesi was a man who believed in luck.

Luck had, however, proved an elusive commodity for a man born deformed, a man whose own parents had looked at him with pity until the day he left home. But now his luck seemed to be turning. If the cops believed he was dead and that they were to blame, then a blow had already been struck against his enemies. With a minimum of effort he could twist the blade in the wound.

Twist the blade, yeah. I like that, he thought. So I follow them. I figure out what they're up to in Pennsylvania—probably tracking down the body to try to clear their own names, he thought. That's what I'd do. And they know how to do it, too.

So it's up to me to make sure they don't clear themselves. Find out what they're trying to prove and then just trip them up here and there, he thought. And maybe I will nab the kid, send ransom notes, teach the brat to say, "Mommy sucks."

Calvesi had never been to Pennsylvania. He was not a man who vacationed much. But now the idea appealed to him.

He went off to the locker room to shower with a strong deodorant soap that he ordered special.

Sam whistled contentedly as he flipped through the card catalog that covered a whole wall in the county clerk's office. Give me a good courthouse any day, he thought. And this, so far as courthouses went, was a good one.

Like everything else around here, it was built—built quite well—of heavy red bricks. A white, weathered concrete keystone in front said the building had been erected in 1908. The cheap-detergent-scrubbed smell of institutions filled the building, a smell that evoked grade school, hospitals, insurance offices.

The colonial style building was three stories high and, though small, laid out like courthouses everywhere. Two superior courtrooms, a handful of smaller courts, a court officers' office, and a criminal clerk's office were on the top two floors. County offices, each one behind its own frosted-glass door, occupied the first floor.

Because it was a county building and therefore a seat of patronage, there was an elevator with an elevator attendant. He dozed in the corner seat of the lift, happy in the saunalike warmth of his office, stirring slightly when Sam and Sara walked by.

Sam and Sara did not need the elevator; their business took them to the first floor. Here was the feeding trough of the investigative reporter, the vast repository of the public record. Eat your fill. No better place to find information fast about a person than your friendly county courthouse. And no better place to start than the Office of the County Clerk, Room 101.

A woman with tight silver spit curls and a pinched expression, who looked like a French poodle walking on hind legs, carried coffee into a glassed-in booth where another public servant sat. He was undoubtedly James L. Miller, county clerk (that's what the small plaque on his desk said). After smiling and setting the coffee mug on Miller's desk, the woman returned to the outer room and clicked over to Sam and Sara, who stood at the counter.

"Can I help you?" she asked in a voice that suggested she really didn't want to.

"Where would we find birth certificates and death certificates, please?" Sara asked in her Really Sweet And Not At All Threatening Voice (she also had a Really Sweet With a Hint of Don't Fuck With Me Voice, a voice more appropriate with elected officials than low-level clerks).

"Who are you with?" the woman asked.

"Excuse me?" Sweet Sara asked.

"You reporters?"

Sara batted her eyes—not cutely, but in the manner of a tiger flicking its tail before charging. Her husband (who knew that she was about to ream this flunky out with a lecture on Public Records: I Have a Right to See Them; Mind Your Own Goddamn Business) quickly intervened.

"No, ma'am, we're not," he said pleasantly. No sense antagonizing her. "Just doing a little academic research." Boring enough.

The woman jabbed a thumb over her shoulder at a hand-lettered sign that was suspended from the ceiling by two guide wires. "Birth and Death Certificates," it said.

"How's about Real Estate?"

She jerked her other thumb over her other shoulder. Sam's eyes glowed as they swept across the lofty room. Throughout the clerk's office, similar signs hung from the ceiling, advertising the various files that were open to the public's inspection. Real Estate. Chattel. Business Licenses. Agricultural Permits. Livestock. Corporations.

"Help yourself," the woman said. Worn out from her exertions, she went back into James L. Miller's cubicle, sat down, and had some coffee.

Five minutes later Sara dropped a quarter into the wheezing municipal copying machine. She pressed the button, and the machine spit out a gray copy of Emil Stoltzfus's birth certificate.

"Born August 19, 1938, to Lucille Stoltzfus, née Kingley, and Earl Stoltzfus," Sam, coming up behind her, read over Sara's shoulder. "That makes him fifty-three. A little young to be our corpse, I'd say."

"Maybe," Sara said. "Of course, our corpse was a midget, and maybe they age faster. Remember the Wizard of Oz? All those munchkins looked old. Stoltzfus could be the guy in the chest. I didn't find a death certificate."

"Office of marriage licenses is in a different building," Sam said. "I checked. Only open between one P.M. and three P.M. on alternating Wednesdays, according to the assistant clerk I rudely interrupted in the middle of a three-week coffee break.

"I struck out on lawsuits. The guy must not be litigious," he continued. "Also on finding business partners. Emil Stoltzfus is not an officer of any company incorporated in this county."

"Now what?" Sara asked. She never had much patience for documents; Sam, however, loved to hang a good story on a paper trail.

"Real Estate and Chattel," Sam said. "Let's see whether he owned any other property and whether it's encumbered."

Mighty libers, thirty-inch-tall notebooks of lined and dated sheets, were filed alphabetically in the metal book racks of the Real Estate and Chattel department. Sam ran his finger across the bindings and stopped at the volume, marked in gold letters, "St."

There were dozens of Stoltzfuses, but only one Stoltzfus stood out like a tombstone: Emil Stoltzfus.

"Wahhhhhh," murmured Sara.

"Whewwww," whispered Sam.

Three full pages listed debts and liens against the farmer. From the farmhouse, to the 100-acre tract, to the tractor, Emil Stoltzfus was a man in hock up to his possibly headless neck.

"One hundred, two, three . . . there's nearly three hundred fifty thousand dollars' worth of debt here," Sara said.

"Seems pretty weird," said Sam.

"Not so unusual," said James L. Miller, who had quietly emerged from his office and was standing behind Sam and Sara.

They looked at him.

"There's a lot of debt out here. The farm business isn't what it was," the clerk said. As he headed off to refill his coffee, he called over his shoulder, "Closing in five minutes, folks. Hope you found what you needed."

SEVENTEEN

Molly, with Baby on her lap, operated a joystick to blow up Nazi ammunition dumps on the very expensive NEC full-color monitor that was, according to Schedule A of the Fishers' tax return, used exclusively for scientific research.

"Oh, cool, they have Rocket Ranger," Sam whispered. Out of professional habit, he and Sara were spying from the bushes outside the Fishers' living room window.

Jake, wearing his reading glasses, was sitting in a corner of the room, flipping through the pages of a thick book. From time to time he picked up a pen to make a note in the margin.

Molly destroyed a zeppelin, which disintegrated colorfully on the screen, accompanied by Baby's delighted preverbal sound effects.

" 'Chapter Ten. The first happiness I knew was in the rented farmhouse of strangers.' "

"I beg your pardon?"

"Baby's diary," Sara said. "She hopes to publish an autobiography when she's old enough to run away."

"Oh, you mean 'Lonely Child: Years of Confinement, Years of Neglect'? I caught her typing it in her crib," Sam said.

They watched Molly enclose Baby's tiny fist in her own over the joystick. Baby looked up at her and smiled lovingly as the Third Reich's premier Panzer division was torched.

" 'I don't even recall the name of the dashing but aloof research scientist with the icy blue eyes and thinning hair. Or his charming wife, the rosy-cheeked matron who held me to her ample bosom and cooed softly as I made the world safe for democracy. Even now I scarcely dare to think it: Were they my real parents?' "

"Stop torturing yourself."

" 'While the people who raised me pursued their own selfish interests—searching out new restaurants, reveling in boiled dinners or a new kind of jerked chicken, neglecting me in their obsessive search for the perfect sausage—the hardworking scientists sneaked me healthful snacks of yogurt and string cheese.' "

" 'If not for them, I probably wouldn't be here today to pen my sad story,' " Sam added just as Jake saw them through the window.

Jake closed the book. Sam squinted and was able to make out the title: "Symbolism and Icons in Amish Culture." Looks like someone's doctoral thesis, Sam thought. No wonder he's such a fascinating conversationalist.

The professor waved, and the evil foster parents skulked away from the window and climbed up onto the porch.

* * *

Idly picking pepperonis off the remaining slices of a pizza, Sam and Sara and Molly watched Jake carefully water a dozen seedling fruit trees he was nursing under a plant lamp in the kitchen. "Doing chores helps him think straight," Molly explained.

"Eating pizza helps me think straight," said Sara, licking a greasy finger.

"But only if you can't get chocolate," said Sam. Sara hoped he wouldn't bring up the mints.

"When she was pregnant, she had a secret cache of After Eight mints," Sam said. "I'd come home and find little paper wrappers all over the apartment. I'd ask about it. I would get no answer. I expected Baby to be born with a severe caffeine addiction."

Sara sat up straight, aimed a dark look at Sam, and said, in her sweetest voice, "What were you about to say, Jake?"

"Well, I was about to say that we have some chocolate mint ice cream in the freezer. But before that, I was thinking that from what you're saying about the mail, I'd say it's a good bet Stoltzfus left home unexpectedly," Jake said. Molly jumped up to set out bowls and spoons.

"Yeah, we just have a hunch," Sam said.

"Why don't you tell the police?" Molly was still worried about being charged as an accessory, Sara thought.

"Because we don't have anything solid to go on," Sam said. "What would we tell them, that we broke into a guy's house and found, uh, let's see, found he wasn't home?"

"We don't want to let the cops know we've been snooping around unless we have something really juicy to divert their attention away from us—like proof that Emil Stoltzfus is running around without any feet or hands or head," Sara said. Molly scooped ice cream into the bowls and passed them around the table.

"Why don't you go ask his relatives if they've seen him?" Jake said.

"What relatives? It looked like he lived all alone, a bachelor."

"You're right, he probably does live by himself," Jake said. "And when I spoke to the deacon, he didn't say anything about relatives. But from what you described of his house, it's obvious he was once married and probably had a family."

Stoltzfus's house was filled with clues, Jake explained, clues screaming out to anybody who knew anything about Amish custom.

The linen towel, for instance.

"Think of it as the Amish equivalent of a diamond engagement ring," Jake said.

"Yeah, yeah, we took the tour," Sam said.

"Did you see a clock in the house? A tall, hand-carved clock?"

"No."

"You know the bridegroom would build a clock for his fiancée, a gift that would stand in their house for the rest of their lives," Jake said.

"We were in all the rooms. But maybe we missed it," Sam said.

"Maybe," Jake said. "But that embroidered towel is a sure sign, as sure as if you'd seen a framed copy of their marriage certificate on the wall."

"So where's the wife now?" Sara asked.

"It's unlikely they divorced—the Amish aren't big on divorce. Maybe she's dead. That towel may have been hanging there, clean and starched, for thirty or forty years, for all we know," Jake said. "But I'll bet you, if he was married, they had kids. Your Old Order Amish families don't practice birth control. Don't believe in it. The average family has about seven kids."

"Seven kids? How does a guy with a wife and a bunch of kids end up living all alone?" Sam asked.

"Alone and unnoticed," Sara said.

"All alone and unnoticed and eating stale funnel cake," Sam mused. "What a way to grow old."

"But how do we track his family when we don't know any names?" Sara asked.

"Next clue," Jake said. "The Bible on the mantelpiece." Any Amish family Bible ought to have an up-to-date family tree in it, he said. It was even likely, Jake mused, that the family record would show Stoltzfus's wife's maiden name and whether she was dead—or just missing, like her husband—as well as the birth dates of any children.

"Too bad you didn't happen to look at the Bible," Jake said.

Yeah, too bad. They were still mulling it over an hour later back at the motel.

"I suppose we really should drop this whole thing," Sam said. "And call Smith. He sounded kind of whiny this morning."

Sara, humming Lonely Child to sleep in the portable crib, didn't answer.

Sam supposed they really should go home. "I hate sleeping in strange beds."

Sara, tucking a fuzzy blanket around the sleeping infant, didn't answer.

Sam supposed he really should discourage Sara from what she was thinking. "We'll end up behind bars."

Sara, punching up the pillows before settling onto her side of the thick mattress, didn't answer.

"I suppose you know we can't just go around breaking into people's houses day after day," Sam said.

Sara didn't answer.

"And exposing Baby to a life of crime."

"Oh, Dutch, what's the difference between breaking and entering once and breaking and entering twice?"

"I vote we call Smith and find out."

"All right, don't think of it as trespassing. Think of it as visiting. Come on. If what Jake told us is true, then we have to go back. And you know if we call Smith, he'll say come home."

"Sara, if we don't go home, it sounds like Graber's going to send a posse after us. We should at least direct Smith to stall."

"Graber. Somebody ought to string up a side of beef across the room from her desk to keep the flies off her," Sara observed.

"We'd need another diversion while we're waiting for the meat to rot."

Sara considered. Baby, dreaming of demolishing computer-generated enemy fighters, sighed. Her even breathing was testimony that she was glad to be in a crib that smelled familiar after an exhausting day spent playing computer games, upholstering furniture, and repairing the motor of a vacuum cleaner ("When does he work on that genetic study, anyway?" Sara had asked Sam as they had driven away from the house, leaving Jake on a stepladder, caulking around the storm windows.)

The Bible seemed to be the best lead they had.

"Jake was a bad influence on you," Sam said, drowsily pulling the vaguely musty blanket up around his neck. "It's cold in here."

"Did Baby just sniffle?" Sara asked worriedly.

"Sound effect. She's dreaming that her tank division just mowed down a regiment of Nazi foot soldiers."

Teetering on the edge of sleep, Sam supposed he would call Smith. In the morning.

EIGHTEEN

If the fuzzy pills on panty hose could emit sparks when rubbed together, Graber would have looked like a rocket blazing down the long corridor toward the crime laboratory. She was propelled by a sheet of white paper she clasped in a chapped fist. It was a note, just two little sentences composed of letters cut out of magazines:

cALvesI waNteD 2 KiLL
tHEm & tHEY kN$_e$w iT wHy r thEy
iN PA noW? sIGnEd a FRiEnd

To Graber, it spelled promotion.

Erbatz was waiting inside the lab, irritation on his face.

"This better be good, Sergeant," he warned her.

It wasn't like Graber to stick her chicken neck out for wringing. She was too ambitious and too smart. If she was going to mysteriously summon her superior to meet her in the crime lab, maybe she really did have something good.

"It's a lead, Lieutenant." She waved the piece of paper. "A note. About Calvesi. From somebody who knows that Calvesi sent them threatening letters from prison. I think this could be our break."

She held the paper out for Erbatz to examine.

"An anonymous note, Graber? I'm late for lunch because you're excited about an anonymous note? You've been watching too many Charlie Chan movies."

Her face fell.

Erbatz relented. "Where'd you get this?"

"In my mail today."

"Addressed to you?"

"Odd, isn't it? Who besides the two of them knew that I'm heading the investigation? This must come from someone with access to them, someone they told about Calvesi's threats. My name hasn't been in the papers," Graber said.

"Well, for starters, everyone in the department knows you're on the case. Everyone you've questioned knows. That Smith guy knows. His secretary knows. After answering your phone calls for nearly a week, Stavropoulos's wife certainly knows. Don't jump to conclusions, Graber."

"Who knows they're back in Pennsylvania?"

"If they are."

"That weasely doorman told me that's where they said they were going," Graber said.

A white-coated lab technician sauntered over and gently used tweezers to pry the sheet of paper from Graber's hand. "We'll need your prints for elimination," he said disapprovingly. "Since you've pawed this thing."

The technician turned to Erbatz. "We'll analyze the

paper, the ink, and the paste," he said. "We'll check for prints other than Sergeant Graber's. We'll send somebody up to get the envelope, so we can test the saliva on the flap and take a close look at the postmark."

"I'll want the report this afternoon," Graber said, too loudly.

The technician looked at Erbatz. "You'll get the report this afternoon, Lieutenant."

"Thanks, Kraussie," Erbatz said. "No real hurry."

Graber flushed.

"Graber, you're a good cop. You know your job. So go do it and stop acting like some rookie." Erbatz started down the hall.

Graber had anticipated his reaction. She waited until she was sure he was gone. Then she walked slowly back to her shabby office, reading a second piece of paper that she pulled from her pocket. Her instincts had been right. Erbatz never would have let her follow up on this one. Only four words were pasted on this second sheet: "prOOf iN tHeir aPT."

An hour later she stepped off the elevator on the ninth floor. The stretch of hallway leading to Sam and Sara's door smelled vaguely of boiled cabbage. A lot of old people in the building, probably. Which could explain why the routine canvass had come up empty: Nobody had seen or heard anything strange on the day the body turned up in the trunk.

Conscious of the possibility of unseen watchers behind the peepholes, Graber knocked lightly on the door. Which shouldn't have opened. But it did. It was unlocked. Forgetting that she considered herself surveilled, Graber pushed the door all the way open. Cautiously she looked inside. Nobody seemed to be home. Late afternoon sun cast shadows on the walls behind the armchairs.

Graber went in. God, the place was clean, she thought. You could eat off these floors. I guess if you don't work for a living, you have to keep busy somehow. She walked through the whole apartment once, getting her bearings, making sure she was alone. And wondering why the door had been open. Were Sam and Sara—or any two New Yorkers, for that matter—really so careless?

Okay, then, proof. What was the proof? And where was the proof? She started in the bedroom, idly opening and closing dresser drawers. About halfway down, she pulled too hard, and a loose drawer fell out, spilling a mound of black elastic things onto the floor. Graber looked at the lingerie with distaste. Bras. Panties. Filmy short gown things. All black.

She averted her eyes. Her glance fell onto the easel in the corner. God, what a horrible image, Graber thought. Some vicious monster with red eyes and a squint. She shuddered, but was fascinated by the pointy chin, the wart-encrusted nose, the mound of hair that crouched above the face. The odd-colored stockings that were bunched up at the thing's knees.

Who could even imagine hair like that? Graber thought, noticing that limp strands were really snakes, their ends evil fanged faces that hissed venom. She must really be a witch, wearing all that tacky black stuff and painting demons. Graber could just picture it, Sara in some see-through black camisole and high heels, dancing around the easel, waving a dripping paintbrush. Now, that ought to be against the law; forget murder.

The kitchen did not seem to hold proof. No pickled heads or hands or feet in the cupboards. Just some smelly, dusty canister labeled "Curry."

Graber was a professional. She searched the nursery: No contraband among the diapers. She checked the bathroom: half a tube of contraceptive jelly, but the diaphragm was missing. Distasteful as she imagined sex could be between those two, she was thankful they practiced birth control. The last thing the world needed were more Amstel-Popkins. She looked in all the closets.

Frustrated, Graber threw herself into the green armchair. Her eyes roamed the room, the bookshelves stuffed to bursting, the Picasso sketch over the sofa, the coffee table battered from repeated infant rammings.

The sun, getting lower, was in her eyes. Graber looked down at the rug, and the glint of a shiny object caught her eye.

She walked over and crouched down. She picked up a gold ID bracelet that was half hidden under one leg of the sofa. She read the name on it: Dominic 12-4-38.

To Graber it spelled proof.

"No one was home but this, and this was in the threshold?" Erbatz, holding the bracelet up to the light on the end of a pencil, looked skeptical. "It's not admissible, Graber."

"Lieutenant, I told you. I went by to question them on my way home. I stopped and talked to the doorman. He said he didn't know if they were there. I knocked. I thought I heard someone say, 'Come in.' The door swung open. And I saw the bracelet, right there on the floor. I never even went inside," Graber said.

"Unlocked. Someone called from inside. Never went in."

"Correct, sir."

Erbatz considered the bracelet, watching it swing back and forth in front of his eyes. "All right, send it down to the lab for prints," he said.

She relaxed. "Yes, sir."

"What else did the doorman say?" Erbatz said.

"One interesting statement. Apparently, while they were carrying the chest up into the apartment, the wife tried to bribe him. She suggested that the chest would be their 'dirty little secret.' The husband tried to slip him some money to get rid of him before they opened the chest."

Erbatz stopped. He looked at her.

"How sure are you that they went to Pennsylvania?"

"The doorman said that on Monday, when he last saw them, they were talking about trying to get to Lancaster County before traffic got heavy."

"Have you asked Lancaster County for assistance?"

"It seems so delicate at this point, Lieutenant. I wanted to ask your advice."

Like hell you did.

"Okay, Graber, go find them."

She blasted off down the hall ahead of him, a furious ball of lumpy clothes headed upstairs to requisition a police car and an unsuspecting assistant. Erbatz, thoughtful, watched her retreating crepe soles.

It sounds right, he thought. I just wish I had an inkling who sent that note.

NINETEEN

"Detective Oudinot, New York City Police Department," said the small man in a neat suit. He had slipped up behind Marlin Bainey, who was hunkered down, tinkering with an industrial-sized electric meat grinder.

Startled, Bainey jammed a screwdriver into his own palm. It was something he would have done sooner or later anyway.

"Goddamn son of a bitch," Bainey said. It sounded more like "cot daim son uff a beetch."

Bainey straightened. "Something's jammed in the damned thing," he said. "Won't grind. So I can't ship out the sausage. Got to get it fixed soon."

Oudinot flipped open his wallet and stuck his badge under Bainey's grit-blackened nose.

"I need to ask you a couple of questions, Mr. Bainey."

Bainey sighed. "I oughta start charging you guys for my time."

The detective smiled and stuck a stick of Juicy Fruit gum in his mouth.

"I won't take up any more of your time than necessary."

Bainey pulled a graying handkerchief from his back pocket and dabbed at the drop of blood on his palm.

Bainey was terrible with tools. Which was a real handicap for someone in the farming business. When your livelihood depended on the speed with which you converted pig into pork, a broken meat grinder was disastrous.

But Bainey had never had much luck fixing things on his own. He started tinkering, unscrewing here, pulling apart there, until the guts of a machine were spread out on the ground before him. Then he stood in front of the whole mess, pushing parts around with his toe, swearing, forgetting what went where. That stage of "repairs" usually lasted a day or two, until Bainey broke down and called the handyman in exasperation.

Anything that needed hammering inevitably resulted in a smashed thumb; anything that needed sawing, a cut finger. His digits—he had all ten, a happy testimonial to his avoidance of power tools—were streaked with scars that looked like melted wax. There was no way Bainey would be able to fix the meat grinder he was manhandling. Not today, not ever. Yet he had been poking and prodding at the metal casing like a badger trying to get at an armadillo.

Now he had an excuse to stop.

"What do you want to know? I told the last bunch the whole story."

The detective took a newspaper clipping from his wallet, unfolded it to show Bainey the photos, and said, "Have you seen these two people?"

"Them again. I told you I already gave the whole story. I never sold them nothing."

"I understand that. My question is, have you seen them lately?"

"Seen them a couple of days ago. Why? They didn't do it, did they? They didn't seem like murderers. Rude, maybe, but not killers. Had a cute kid."

"Do you know where I could find them?"

"No, I do not." Bainey was getting impatient.

"Just a couple more questions, Mr. Bainey, and I'll be gone. What did they want from you?"

"Asked me some questions about the Amish. I told them to see the professor."

"What professor?"

"Fisher. Jake Fisher. Lives out in the country. Why don't you ask him?"

The detective smiled. "I will." On his way back through the barn, the detective spit his gum into his hand, rolled it into a neat little ball, and pitched it into a box of buttons near the doors.

The place didn't seem nearly so creepy at high noon, Sara thought. She sidled up to Stoltzfus's kitchen table, careful not to touch the plate of funnel cake, turned quite hard by now, or the glass of milk, which had formed a skin thick enough to support a bouncing quarter.

She walked across the sticky linoleum and stopped in front of the embroidered towel. She lightly fingered the fine stitches on its border.

"Note to myself," she said aloud. "Remind husband that non-Amish women who never got diamond rings might grow resentful."

Sam was in the living room, using his portable barbecue tongs (you never know when you're going to come across some vegetables that need grilling) to lift the Bible gently off the mantel and into a plastic freezer bag.

"Note to myself," Sara heard him mutter. "Replace wife with less greedy model."

She wandered into the living room. "Why would an adult drink milk?" she asked. "That is the real mystery here."

Sam sealed the zip top and folded up his tongs.

"What is this with the tongs, Sam?"

"Fingerprints," he said a little sheepishly.

"What, we're going to read through it using tongs? Page by page tonging through Genesis? We'll never get to Deuteronomy."

"We don't need to, Frenchie. The family tree is near the beginning. I want to preserve the crime scene as much as possible."

"Please, don't talk to me about—"

They froze. They both heard it.

"A car?" Sara whispered.

The whine got louder. Wordlessly, they dropped to their knees and crawled to the front window for confirmation. They lifted their heads just high enough to sneak a glance through the glass. They saw a dirty green Ford LTD pull off the road. It made an ominous crunching sound as the wheels turned onto the dirt rut that Stoltzfus called a driveway.

Halfway between the road and the house the car slowed, then stopped, like a horse sniffing the air for rattlesnakes before trotting into an unfamiliar valley. Sam and Sara could see two people in the front seat. They seemed to be talking.

"Men?" Sara whispered.

"Can't tell."

"Stoltzfus?"

"If so, there goes our theory," Sam said.

Apparently Sam and Sara did not smell like rattlesnakes, because the LTD was once again moving toward the house.

"The back door?" Sara whispered.

"No time. We'd get nabbed trying to sneak out." Sam thought about the Range Rover, which he had discreetly parked behind the dairy barn, out of view from the road. No way could they drive the car across a field without attracting attention. And the driveway was blocked.

They both realized it at the same time: There's nowhere to hide in an Amish house. No closets to climb in. No overstuffed sofas or chairs to crouch behind. No long, dark hallways to lurk in. No beds with dust ruffles to crawl under. Plainness, as a decorating aesthetic, provided no cover.

"The pantry."

He nodded. They scooted away from the window and then trotted, hunched over like identical Groucho Marxes (*sans* cigars), through the living room into the kitchen. They headed for the walk-in pantry. They opened the door—and gasped. The storage area had been overturned. A fifty-pound sack of flour spilled onto the floor. Smashed Ball jars of preserved fruits and vegetables were crashed in the corner. Preserved tomatoes, pickled corn, and apple butter were smeared on the walls like an overturned salad bar. The pantry smelled putrid.

A car door closed. Then another. They squeezed into the pantry, left the door open a slit, and hunkered down in the food muck.

"Let's make out," Sara whispered.

Sam put his arm around her.

"I'm cramped," Sara said.

"At least we have a good view," Sam said, settling the bag with the Bible on the cold floor between his feet, where he could find it in the dark.

"You have a good view. I have a butt full of corn relish," Sara said.

They heard a scraping at the front door and then the creak of it swinging open.

Wait a minute, Sam thought. That windbag Fisher said the custom is for everybody to use the kitchen door in an Amish house. This must not be Stoltzfus coming home.

They heard footsteps creak across the wide planks of the living room floor. There were two sets of feet, one pair that clomped sternly ahead and a second set that followed unevenly, limping as if the walker were dragging a heavy bag of meal.

Sam squinted as the men attached to the feet came into view through the kitchen doorway. Sam could see two burly backs standing by the fireplace. The tall back wore a long black overcoat and a fedora. The short back, under a camel-colored coat, was oddly twisted. The limper.

"You take the living room. I'll do the upstairs," a voice said. A grunt of assent followed. "Do a good job."

Immediately the noises of a room being searched filled the house. Drawers were dumped onto the floor, papers were rifled through, the mattress on the sofa was overturned. Sara imagined she heard the sound of a knife slitting the fabric of the sofa.

"Not here," the limper growled, his voice filled more with fear than with anger. "Shit."

"Got to be," the fedora yelled from upstairs. A chest of drawers crashed to the floor above them. "Keep looking."

"Not here, you stupid fuck," whispered the limper. He pried up floorboards with a screwdriver. Each board came up with a heavy creak, then a sigh. Ten minutes passed. The fedora came down the stairs.

"Well?" he asked.

"I looked everywhere," said the limper.

"We're going to have to figure out some way to get my

fucking money back. No money means no paycheck for you, boy-o." The fedora was not happy.

"You want me to toss the place again?" The limper knocked over a small table, overturned a ladder-back chair. "I don't see nothing," he said. "Maybe in the kitchen." He started to limp toward the kitchen.

Sara squeezed Sam's arm with one hand and began to move the other gently over the dark surfaces in the pantry, her touch as light as if she were reading braille as her fingertips encircled the neck of a ketchup bottle.

Sara heard the sliding steps get closer to the pantry door. She heard a hand turn the doorknob. She pressed her shoulder tightly against Sam.

"Forget about it," said the fedora.

"No more tossing?" The limper was disappointed.

"No, it's definitely not here. We searched the pantry before and found nothing. Let's get out of here."

The fedora turned to scan the room. Eyes as bloodshot as a copy editor's darted into the corners, into the kitchen, into the dark hole of the pantry doorway. His face was very pale. Sam and Sara started; the last time they had seen that man, they had paid him cash for a corpse.

"Yeah. Fine," the limper said. He strode from Sam's view, out the front door. Squidly's eyes raked the room again. His pupils were dead flies suspended in fake ice cubes. He slammed the door shut behind him.

They heard the LTD's door slam and the car's engine turn over. They heard the whine that meant there was not enough steering column fluid, as the driver turned the vehicle around in the rut. They heard the engine grow fainter.

Only when the sound was gone did Sam and Sara creep, cautiously, from the pantry into the kitchen.

"Let's get out of here," Sam said, gently disengaging

Sara's fingers from the ketchup bottle she had forgotten she held.

"That was the guy, Sam."

"Let's get out of here, Frenchie," he repeated.

Sara looked a little pale, even for her. "We should follow them," she said.

"We don't even know which way they went."

They went outside and, out of habit, crept toward their car.

"In the movies we'd follow them."

"In the movies they'd have found us and hacked us up with a chain saw," Sam said.

"You're thinking of *Scarface*," she said.

"I'm thinking of Squidface."

They got in the Range Rover, and as Sam was trying to remember which pocket held his keys, they heard the sound of the engine again.

From their vantage behind a big evergreen, they saw the LTD come over a rise and drive toward the house. It did not slow as it neared the driveway. It did not turn in.

"What's going on?" Sara said.

"They may be scary. But they aren't too smart," Sam said. "They must have turned the wrong way when they pulled out."

The Range Rover pulled out from behind the dairy barn in pursuit.

TWENTY

Two very dangerous murderers from the big city were loose in Pennsylvania, roaming the peaceful valley, and threatening the simple country folk. The innocent-eyed representatives of the local law should respond. Broadcast the monsters' license plate number far and wide. Warn local innkeepers that the urban marauders might be holed up, planning their next caper.

"I see," said Lt. David Noonan. "Very interesting, Sergeant Graber."

This yahoo was not showing the proper concern. Or respect.

"No, I don't believe you do see," Graber said. "If you did see, you would be on the radio right now, alerting your squad cars—you do have squad cars, don't you?"

"Squad cars and sirens, excuse me, si-reens, and guns, even," Noonan said. And manners, he thought.

He indicated, with a nod, a long line of blue cruisers parked along the one-way street in front of police headquarters. The driver's side of each car was adorned by a bright red rose, a reference to Lancaster, "The Red Rose City." It was one of the many charming details about the city that Graber had overlooked in her haste to reach headquarters by two. She had noticed and been annoyed by the inconveniences of one-way streets named after fruits. "Lime, Lemon, Orange, Plum," she muttered disgustedly. "Bunch of fruits."

She had driven past the Lancaster Cleft Palate Clinic, only three blocks from police headquarters, but had not stopped to wonder how a city this small could support a clinic that catered to such a specialized deformity.

"They drive a Range Rover," Graber said. "Tell your officers to expect blaring music."

Noonan, careful not to smile, nodded and wrote "loud music" on the notepad in front of him.

"Let's go over that description again," Noonan said. "We want to be sure we've got it right."

Anyone other than Graber might have detected a note of sarcasm. But all she saw, when she glanced up sharply, was a bland face in aviator glasses, a face that looked as if it were always battling conflicting urges to smile or say, "For Pete's sake."

Graber sighed audibly. These chuckleheads. Here she was, finally, after a harrowing three hours on interstate highways, trying to save these silly people from themselves. Offering them partial credit for the collar. Not raising her voice. And the result?

"We're wasting valuable time," Graber said.

"The description?" Noonan prompted her.

"Husband is overweight, like a big hairy tree trunk.

Shabby clothes, blue work shirts, and corduroy pants like a cheap imitation of *This Old House*. Smug. Dirty, wild hair. Scruffy thicket of a beard. Intrusive dark eyes."

Noonan wrote on his notepad: medium height, 180 pounds, brown hair, brown eyes, beard.

"Wife is a witchy little thing, skinny insect arms and legs, stringy dark hair, favors black Spandex, eyes usually sunken, probably from a hangover."

Noonan wrote on his notepad: short, 100 pounds, black hair, black eyes.

"They should be considered armed and dangerous." Even Graber was beginning to wonder if she was getting a little carried away.

"With a baby?" Noonan did not write down anything.

"Part of their cover."

"Ingenious," Noonan said.

"I don't think you understand the gravity of this case," Graber said. "These two people are prime suspects in a murder. A vicious murder. Although the body was badly mangled, as I told you, we have evidence that leads us to believe they snuffed an ex-con, a midget—"

"You mean a dwarf?"

"Whatever."

"Hmmm. Now that is interesting. Very common here among the Amish, you know. Probably because of recurring intramarriage. An interesting study a few years back traced all known cases to Samuel King and wife, a couple of settlers who came here in the mid-eighteenth century."

"Fascinating." Graber hated to be interrupted.

"Yup. We have two kinds—those suffering from Cartillage-Hair Hypoplasia and the Ellis-van Creveld Syndrome."

"Ellis-van . . ."

"Yeah. Really rare. Six fingers. More than half the known cases in the whole world are right here in the Pennsylvania Dutch country. You feeling okay?" Noonan noticed Graber turn suddenly pale.

A smooth-faced, uniformed officer popped her head around the corner of Lieutenant Noonan's open door, looked at the two seated facing each other across his desk, and said, "Oh, is the detective from New York here? Duty sergeant has a message for her. I'll go get it."

"Thank you, Morris," Noonan said.

He looked back at Graber.

She crossed her ankles primly. "In addition to the midget angle, we have some fairly convincing forensic evidence. The victim was of Italian descent. Analysis of the stomach contents revealed a sweet, doughy substance—possibly deep fried—and powdered sugar. Indicative of an Italian pastry known as bomboloni—"

"Funnel cake," Noonan said. "Sounds like funnel cake to me. That's a real common dessert—or breakfast—around here, particularly among the Amish. Delicious, by the way."

Graber frowned.

"Really," she said. "I don't think this is helping. We're talking about a victim who fits the description of a reputed hit man, a midget they killed. And then dressing the victim in what would normally be considered Amish garb. White shirt. Dark pants. But there's an indication that they dressed him after he died and handled him clumsily. One of the suspenders on his pants was missing."

"One suspender, huh?" Noonan pulled a lanyard attached to a key chain from his desk drawer and idly twirled it. "One suspender? Was the other one broken or was there only one to begin with?"

"What are you talking about, one suspender? Who wears only one?" Graber's voice was cold enough to flash-freeze the ink in the pen Noonan held.

"You might want to talk to some of the Bremmers about

that. They're an Old Order Amish sect, and they wear only one suspender. I imagine there's even some dwarf among them, and I imagine they also eat some funnel cake now and then," Noonan said. "Why didn't you tell us this before?"

Morris came back into the office. "Here it is, Sergeant. A call from your precinct."

Graber snatched the pink memo slip out of the officer's hand and scanned it. A smile slowly spread across her lightly whiskered lips.

"Good luck," she said. "We got a tip that the suspects we're looking for have been staying with a Dr. Jake Fisher, in Ephrata. I have an address here."

"Where did the tip come from?"

Graber looked again at the message. "No indication here. Probably my partner, Stavropoulos. An excellent street cop."

Noonan looked at the piece of paper Graber thrust in his face. He pinched the bridge of his nose between his thumb and forefinger, cutting off the flow of blood and momentarily holding off the sinus headache that was a frequent side effect of irritation. He had the urge to moan, "For Pete's sake." He stifled it.

"Shall we go, Lieutenant Noonan? Or, if you'd rather stay, perhaps I could trouble you for directions?"

"We're at your disposal, Sergeant. Ephrata's about a half hour from here. And I have a pretty good idea where to find Fisher's house."

"Was that thing airlifted in from Omaha sometime after the war?" Sara asked, staring at the blue trim (theme paint?) and gray stone front of the old building. She reached behind her to the backseat to get the plastic-wrapped Bible.

"Hmmm." Sam was more interested in the scene on which his binoculars were trained, Fedora and Limper locking up their car and heading into the lobby.

"No, dear, that gray stone and architectural style really is more indicative of southeastern Pennsylvania in the early part of the twentieth century," Sara answered herself.

"Hmmm."

The Inn at Blue Ball was larger than the boxy miniature buildings that hobby shops stock for customers who are designing model railroads. But adjusting for scale, it was easy to imagine the hotel sitting beside some *O* gauge track under the shade of a little plastic elm tree. From their vantage point across the street, Sam sat in the driver's seat, looking through binoculars.

"Can you see anything werr-r-r-ry in-ter-restink through those field glasses, *mein herr?*"

"I can see Pennsylvania license plate number A-10-SHN."

She wrote it down in his notebook.

"You see anything else interesting?"

"I can see the outline of a holster under Limper's jacket."

Sara opened the plastic bag and, holding it by two corners, eased the Bible out onto her lap. "Sara, use the tongs!" Sam said.

"Sara, use the tongs!" she imitated in her Sam's-whiny-voice. She looked down at the dog-eared book without opening it. "They were rooting around on the mantel. Maybe they were after his Bible?" she mused. "But why? I doubt they're interested in the family tree."

The two men went inside the inn. Sam lowered the binoculars. "Quit tampering with the evidence. We've got work to do," he said. "We need to figure out who those two are before we do anything else. We can hardly direct the police to arrest someone known only as Squidly."

Reluctantly Sara slid the Bible back into its bag.

They got out of the car, which was parked, as inconspicuously as one can park a Range Rover along a fairly busy Route 30. They dodged traffic to cross the street to where the Ford was parked.

Inside the car, on the dashboard, they could see some mimeographed photos of furniture, stapled together. Next to it was a yellow sheet of paper advertising "Dietrich's Auction House. Winter Sale. Real Amish Collectibles."

"They didn't strike me as the collectibles type," Sam said.

"Is that a guest registration form peeking out underneath?" Sara said.

Sam leaned close to the window, his breath melting the frost that was beginning to coat the tinted glass.

"Can't see their names," he said. "But it looks like they're in Room 48."

"Wait here," Sara said.

Inside, she glanced around the lobby, obviously looking for someone she was supposed to meet. There was no one else waiting.

Sara looked at her watch. She scanned the lobby again. She walked up to the desk clerk, who had been watching since she came in the front door.

"Hi. Can I help you?" he asked.

"I hope so." She smiled. "I'm meeting my father here for dinner. But he must have forgotten and overslept again. Do you think you could call his room? John Miller."

"Of course," the clerk said. "John Miller." He flipped through a stack of registration forms.

"I don't see any Millers," he said.

"Room 48," Sara said helpfully.

"Room 48." The clerk went through the cards again. He was puzzled. "Are you sure? I don't have a John Miller in 48."

"No, he definitely said Room 48. I just spoke with him this morning. Room 48. John Miller."

The clerk looked through his registration cards again. "Room 48," Sara said helpfully.

"I don't see any John Miller registered in the hotel. I have two gentlemen registered in 48, a Mr. Merle Otis and a Mr. Jeffrey Thomson."

"Oh, dear," Sara said, leaning over the counter to check the spellings on the card. "Is there a John Miller expected?"

She fumbled in her purse, searching for the envelope on which she had written her father's room number.

"That room is booked to the same party through Monday. In fact . . . I don't show any reservation for a John Miller at all." The clerk was flipping through another stack of cards.

"Oh, dear. I'd better call Mother," Sara said. "There must be a mixup. Maybe I'm at the wrong hotel."

The clerk looked up, still puzzled, in time to see the front door close very softly.

She found Sam outside at a pay phone. He cupped his hand over the mouthpiece. "Motor Vehicles," he said. "They say a 1985 Ford LTD with the same plates is registered to a Jeffrey Thomson, DOB 11-6-50. Six feet one inch tall. Brown hair, eyes. Pittsburgh address. No violations."

"Have him check Merle Otis, that's o-thomas-i-samuel," she said."

"Rob, can you check this name for me?" Sam said into the phone.

Sara wandered off a few steps and peered up at the fourth floor of the hotel. She could have sworn she saw someone staring from behind the white curtain on the third window from the left.

Sam repeated the words he heard over the phone. "Merle Otis, DOB 9-3-43, license suspended for DWI, last known address a Pittsburgh PO box. Thanks." He hung up.

"Now what?" Sara asked. "The police?"

"Maybe," Sam said. "But I can't think straight on an empty stomach."

"Okay," a quick bite. And then back to Jake's to get Baby. I don't want her picking up any of his bad habits."

TWENTY-ONE

To say that Sam was "eating" a grilled sticky bun would be to describe accurately, in a biological sense, the action that he was about to take. But that description would fail to capture the essence of the moment. Man and sticky bun stood, bun in hand, in an uncrowded aisle of the Shillington Farmer's Market. Sam's eyes were as glazed as the warm caramel-coated, pecan-studded, fist-sized roll they were fixed on. Was it Sam's imagination? Or did the bun seem to beckon him, to call out his name . . . Sssam. Ssssam.

He took a quick, delicate nibble.

And then a deeper bite.

And a third, the coup de grace, pressing the dough all the way into his mouth, his salivary glands working like the insides of a brushless car wash. Caramel dripped on his lips, lingered on his mustache. Sticky bun and man had become one. It was the kind of bond that few could really appreciate, let alone experience.

And it was only an appetizer.

Sam sighed and looked for his wife, who was standing at a nearby stall on tiptoe, trying to stare over the shoulder of a woman with a beehive hairdo. Sara was at the rear of a small crowd of people—good people, Sam thought in glowy post-sticky-bun reverie—watching an Amish baker as he twisted pretzel dough.

The baker dipped the raw pretzels, one by one, into a deep vat of steaming lard, watching the fat bubble around them until they turned brown and barely crusty on the outside. The smell of golden fried dough, dipped quickly in melted butter to form a glaze before the pretzel cooled, had attracted a hearty knot of onlookers, dedicated eaters who laughed in the face of cholesterol. They had lined up, dollars in hand, with the steely determination of Soviets buying black-market toilet paper.

"I can't see anything," Sara complained. "Dionne Warwick is blocking my view."

Sam licked his fingers.

"You have a pecan in your beard," Sara told him.

"Where?" He was scandalized.

"Just dangling," she said.

She turned her attention to the catalog she held, the mimeographed pages from Dietrich's Auction House, which they had picked up on their way to the market. "Hmmm, this would really look good by our front door," she said, poking a finger at a sturdy oak coatrack.

Sam nodded, his eyes on the baker. This is poetry, he thought, sheer poetry the way he so expertly crisps up the outside while keeping the inside soft and doughy. And piping hot. A pretzel is composed of mere flour and water. Mere. A sonnet is composed of mere words.

He thought he might buy a pretzel, after a second sticky bun.

Sara flipped to another page. "The coatrack would look especially good with this wicker chair next to it."

Sam nodded. He was thinking about what rhymes with pretzel: pret-ZEL . . . good SMELL . . . William TELL . . . On my way to work I bought a pretZEL; I lost my grip and down it FELL; Covered in grit 'twas a vision of HELL . . .

"The two aren't expected to fetch more than fifteen hundred dollars together."

Sam shook off his musings with an effort, wondering if this is how Shakespeare felt when Mrs. Shakespeare burst into his study in the middle of some really important iambic pentameter to demand that he go slug rats in the root cellar.

"A tidy sum," Sara said. "Maybe we could cash in one of Baby's college accounts." She circled the description of the coatrack.

Sam clutched at his chest.

"Or sell off your old pizza oven and extra smoker. You never smoke meats anymore, anyway."

Sam made a strangled noise from somewhere behind his beard.

She looked up from the catalog.

"I think we should definitely bid on the coatrack," she said. "It has a real Arts and Crafts feel to it. Solid."

"Sara." Sam decided to try reasoning with her.

"You're right," she said.

"Thank you." He was pleased. Reasoning had worked.

"We really could use the chair more."

"Sara!"

" 'Sara, use the tongs,' " she mimicked.

They moved away from the pretzel stall and headed toward bulk goods. Sara wanted to see if the popcorn here was cheaper than the five pounds they had bought at the Shady Maple IGA; they planned a kernel comparison test based on size, roundness, and depth of hue.

She stuck the auction catalog into her purse. "So why would Thomson and Otis go to a furniture auction? I don't really see them falling all over themselves to snap up American primitives," Sara said.

"Beats me," Sam said. "That catalog sure doesn't give us any better idea about who those guys are. Or what they were after at Stoltzfus's house. Or whether they killed him."

"Or know who did."

"Or know who did," Sam agreed. "They're from Pittsburgh. Maybe they're in town for this auction. I don't know."

"We're not at a dead end, are we?" Sara asked. "Maybe we should toss their room at the hotel."

"Too risky."

"Maybe we should just tail them for a while. They're here until Monday, according to the hotel clerk," Sara said.

"I don't know about tailing them," Sam said. "That stuff never works in real life."

"So what does work in real life?"

"I think we should pursue a different tack for a while," Sam said. "All the easy leads seem to have dried up in this direction."

"What's the other angle?" Sara asked.

"Stoltzfus himself. We need to check out that family tree. And talk to his wife. And figure out why those cheap imitations of Peter Lorre and Sydney Greenstreet were searching his house."

"Maybe they wanted the Bible. Maybe it's an antique book," Sara said. "Maybe they're book collectors and it's a rare book and it has something to do with that antiques auction. Or maybe I'm babbling."

They walked out of the warmth and across the parking lot, the smell of fresh pretzels lingering on their coats.

Sam opened the back of the Rover and loaded their shopping bag full of apple butter, fresh peanut butter, popcorn, and homemade relish. He opened the door on the passenger's side. He climbed in. Sara, in the driver's seat, fastened her seat belt and popped the hatch that sat like a coffee table between the two bucket seats. Inside were road maps, diaper wipes, pencils, notebooks, and back issues of *The Thin Man*. She moved her finger down a stack of CDs.

"Tito Puente?" Sam asked.

"Unless you're in the mood for that samba collection."

Sam reached for his tongs. "We need to look at this Bible more closely," he said.

Sara pushed the driver's seat all the way forward. She adjusted the mirrors. She pumped the gas pedal. The sound of Brazilian sambas thudded out of the four speakers.

Sam had begun to tong through the Bible.

"Here's the family tree, all right." He sounded disappointed.

"What's wrong?" Sara pulled out.

"Husband, Emil Stoltzfus, born August 19, 1938, like we already knew from his birth certificate," Sam read. "Married Ella Lieber, born May 11, 1939."

"So?"

"She died two years ago."

"Another dead end?" Sara sounded tired.

"Actually, maybe not. They seem to have had five children: Jonas, Lucas, Ruth, Mary, and Anne."

"Jonas Stoltzfus? I've seen that name on four mailboxes and one wagon repair shop sign just while we've been driving around," Sara said. She made a sharp left turn from the parking lot. She did not look in the mirror to check if the sound of screeching tires behind her indicated real distress on the part of the motorist she had just cut off.

"I think we need to consult Jake again," Sam said. "He found out Stoltzfus's name for us from that deacon. Maybe he can go back to his source and ask about the kids. Now that we have their names. Or maybe we can do the asking."

He flipped through a few more pages. "I still don't see why Thomson and Otis would be after this Bible, though," he said. "They looked like good boys who had already memorized their verse for the week."

The car in front of Sara stopped at a red light, forcing her to brake. She watched Sam reseal the plastic bag. The light turned green, and Sara honked immediately.

As Sam reached behind him to put the Bible on the backseat, a sheet of white paper fluttered from his lap onto the floor.

"Clue!" Sara shrieked. She jerked the wheel sharply, almost prompting a motorcycle and a van behind her to collide as she pulled onto the shoulder of the road.

Sam scooped up the paper and unfolded it.

It was a receipt, handwritten, for several items of furniture Stoltzfus had sold to Farm Salvage two weeks before.

"'Dresser, $50. Footstool, $5. Table, $25. Clock, $100. Two chairs, $10 apiece,'" Sam read. "Shall I go on?"

"He knew Marlin Bainey? It sure raises more questions." Sara clearly had been expecting something along the lines of Rosebud the Sled. "Maybe there's a message written on there in invisible ink."

"No," Sam said, slowly turning the receipt over in his hands. "I don't think so. I think this is the whole clue."

"We'll need a clue to figure out the clue," Sara complained.

"Maybe," Sam said, reading over the list of items to himself.

TWENTY-TWO

"Open up, police," Graber called, pounding on the cheap aluminum door at Jake's house. "Open up in there. Official business."

Noonan, standing behind her, rolled his eyes. He felt as if he had been transported in a time machine into the middle of a lesser episode of *Starsky and Hutch.* Graber really seemed to favor squealing tires. And pounding on doors. And now that he thought about it, her wardrobe did kind of resemble David Soul's during the mid-seventies.

"Sergeant Graber," Noonan said gently, "I think you can stop pounding."

"I want to give the subjects fair warning that we're—" Graber said, turning toward him just as Noonan shook hands with Jake Fisher, who had come up onto the stoop behind them.

"Professor, how are you?" Noonan said. "I'm Lieutenant Noonan from the Lancaster Police Department."

"Pleased to meet you."

"No, the pleasure is mine, Professor. I heard you lecture over at the community college about cultural differences among the different Amish districts."

"Ah, yes, that," Jake said. "I didn't mean to sneak up on you. I called to you, but I guess you couldn't hear over the commotion."

The two men looked at Graber.

"Are you Jacob Fisher, a.k.a. The Professor?" she demanded.

"Yes to the first part of the question. Sometimes, but only to my undergraduate students, to the second," Jake said. "How can I help you?"

"We have reason to believe you are consorting with felons and may therefore be considered an accomplice to a serious crime, unless you cooperate," Graber said, pulling out her laminated Miranda card.

"Goodness," said Jake as the color drained from his face. "Am I under arrest? What did I do?"

"*Nyahh,*" said Noonan. He nudged Graber aside and walked into the front hall. The sergeant followed. "We just have a few questions. Trying to find some folks missing out of New York City. Hey, got any coffee, Doc?"

"Of course," Jake said. "Please. Come in, sit down. I'd be happy to answer any questions." He looked nervously at Graber. "You're from New York City, but not born there, right? That harsh accent is softened a bit by, say, growing up in Syracuse? Your manner, however, is pure Queens."

Graber colored. "Listen, buddy—"

"Jake Fisher, this is Detective Sergeant Evelyn Graber,"

Noonan said. "I don't think you've been properly introduced. She is attached to the New York City homicide squad and is here on official police business, hoping to locate two, er, possible suspects connected to a murder. We thought you might be of help."

"Murder most foul, eh? My, my. I don't know how I could help you, but of course, as I said, I'd be happy to answer your questions."

Jake gestured for them to sit in the beat-up armchairs in front of the fireplace where some logs were burning cheerfully. He fetched cups from the kitchen and a half-filled carafe from the Mr. Coffee.

"This is the first time I've ever been questioned by the police," Jake told Graber as he tamped down some tobacco into one of his pipes.

"How interesting," she said, pulling open a brown vinyl briefcase and extracting a legal-sized notepad and a small manila envelope. From the envelope she removed two Xerox copies of New York State driver's licenses. The photographs from the licenses were bordered in yellow-overlining.

"We have information that you've been secreting these two perps—"

"Perps?"

"Samuel Popkin and Sara Amstel. Do you know where they are?" Graber handed the copies to Fisher. He gazed for a few seconds at the Xeroxes, then frowned and handed them back to Graber.

"Well, yes, I must confess I have met these people. They came to my house, asked a few questions about the Amish. I couldn't help them."

"How odd," Graber said. "We received a report that their expensively garish foreign jeep has been seen parked in your driveway—a number of times in the past week."

"Sorry," said Jake. "The closest to expensively garish

that we get around here is my '84 Volvo station wagon, Sergeant. Has air-conditioning, which my wife considers a luxury on a poor, untenured professor's salary."

Noonan stood up. "The report may have been a mistake," he said. "But if you hear of or from these people again, please call me immediately. They are suspected in a serious crime."

"You can count on my total cooperation, Lieutenant," Jake said, showing them to the door. "By the way, who's been saying that these people have been parked at my house?"

"Confidential informant," Graber said.

"I thought it was an anonymous tip," Noonan said.

"I really can't say any more," Graber said.

A quarter mile away, on the road that led to Jake's house, Dominic Calvesi watched through binoculars as the police officers shook hands with Jake Fisher, got into the red-rose bedecked cruiser, and drove away. He lowered the binoculars and muttered an obscure Italian oath.

The following day, Sunday, was not a day of rest. Graber set up a command center at the desk next to Noonan's and spent the morning haranguing Stavropoulos, via long distance, over the delay in obtaining Calvesi's childhood medical records from a long-retired Brooklyn physician. Noonan, unnerved by the unexpected out-of-town company, cut short his morning basketball game and invented a reason to come into the office, where he hunched in his chair and pretended to catch up on paperwork.

Had Graber been concentrating less on making Stavropoulos miserable and more on the view outside Noonan's window, she might have noticed a Range Rover with New York plates drive past police headquarters at precisely 11:31 A.M. She might have been able to catch up with Sam and Sara that day—and thereby avert at least one more death. But her attention never wavered from the specific task at hand, which was to get her partner to do some real investigating, for once. "If his father said he broke his leg when he was in high school, there has simply got to be an X-ray somewhere, Stavropoulos," she said into the phone. "I don't care if it's Sunday. I want you to call every emergency room in Brooklyn. Find those records."

So Sam and Sara drove down East Chestnut and turned left, oblivious of the nude-colored menace. Half an hour later, well north of town, they pulled into a muddy parking area, conspicuous for having the only combustion engine in sight. Horses harnessed to empty black carriages surrounded them. From inside the sturdy frame farmhouse, a hundred feet away, came the sound of many voices singing a simple hymn in German. Even Sara felt a little funny about disrupting the peaceful gathering.

She thought they should sit quietly, at least until the hymn ended. They could sit in the car and wait for the members of the Bremmer sect to file out into the yard in groups divided by gender, youngest leading the way.

"No need to barge in," she said.

Sam looked at her, amazed. Was this the same woman who had plotted, as they drove past open land and low barns, to rush in through the Beilers' front door, clutching a shawl-wrapped Baby and pleading for a doctor to "see to the little one"? The same woman who had suggested setting a small fire in the barn to create a diversion that would enable them to approach Deacon Schmidt "naturally"?

"After all," said Sara, the voice of calm, "how much longer can it go on? They started at nine."

Jake, who had given them directions and stern warnings not to interrupt the Bremmers' worship, had said the service probably would end about midday. ("Makes sense," Sam had said. "I have as much respect for God as the next guy, but I

154

wouldn't pray through a meal." But Jake had cautioned: "Don't expect them to give in to hunger pangs; the Amish pass a plate of cookies around the room more often than Catholics pass a collection plate.")

Now Sam and Sara watched their breath fog the inside of the windshield. "Let's go over it again," Sam said.

"Sam, we've rehearsed it a thousand times."

"Sara."

Sara stuck out her jaw. "I'm-sorry-to-bother-you-Deacon-Schmidt-but-I'm-looking-for-a-branch-of-my-fam—" She stopped. "Come on, I know what to say. Don't you trust me?"

The last time Sam had trusted her, Sara had ended up browbeating an eighty-year-old widow. She had been planning to interview a number of elderly tenants for a story about landlords who unleashed pit bulls in the hallways to convince renters to vacate rent-controlled apartments. Arguably, the woman's stroke had been the perfect kicker to the story. But just as arguably, Sara's blunt questions might have been a contributing factor.

"Of course I trust you," Sam lied.

"Then let's go," Sara said, opening the car door as a stream of black-hatted, pale-faced men trickled out the front door and into the yard. "Jake said this would be our window of opportunity—while they're setting up the tables to eat."

Up at the house a small group of men—all were wearing one suspender—surrounded a tall man who was speaking in a low, even voice. In one hand he held a hymnal. In his other hand he held the hat he had just retrieved from a pile on the porch.

"Deacon Schmidt?" Sara sounded timid. In her arms Baby clutched a damp Pengie and smiled wide enough to pop a dimple. The deacon, who had no way of knowing that all men with beards and pleasant modulation reminded Baby of her father, smiled back.

"Hello, little baby," he said. Then he looked at Sara, and the smile was replaced by obvious confusion at seeing a woman in a miniskirt and black high-top sneakers among the sober throng in the Beilers' front yard.

"Deacon, my name is Sara Stoltzfus," Sara said. "This is my daughter, Heidi."

Heidi? Where did she come up with this stuff, Sam wondered. Next, she'll be telling him that we climb around the Alps in *liederhosen*. She's even capable of belting out "Edelweiss" to the assembled crowd, if she thinks it will get them to open up, he thought. Sara, please, he resorted to mental telepathy, please be careful. They may speak German, but they don't know it from yodeling.

"This is my husband, Fritz," Sara said.

Fritz cut in. "We're sorry to bother you, Deacon, but we've come a long way. We were driving through Lancaster and decided to stop when we realized how close we were to the valley where some distant cousins are supposed to be living. We hope you can tell us where to find them."

"Ja. We've been looking for a long time," Sara said.

"Let's go inside, where it's warmer," Deacon Schmidt said, leading them into the house, which smelled of scalloped potatoes and ham—Sam saw it being ladled, steaming, into bowls.

In the kitchen Mary Beiler, who had been directing men to set up a long table here and women to set down apple pies there, patted a loose strand of hair up under her organdy cap and said, "Please, won't you sit down? You'll be more comfortable."

They settled on a bench in the corner. "What a happy baby," the deacon said, returning "Heidi's" wet grin. "Who are your cousins?"

"A long-lost branch of the Stoltzfus family," Sara said. "We're having a family reunion in Wichita—that's where we live, Kansas—next summer, and we wanted to invite them. If we can find them."

"About one out of every four people around here is named Stoltzfus," the deacon said.

"Ja, we know, but the name's very rare in Wichita," Sara said.

Rare in Wichita? What was she talking about, Fritz wondered. Saying, "Ja" was rare in Wichita. This free association business had to stop.

"Do you know anything more about your relatives?" the deacon asked.

"Just that they belong to the Bremmer sect," Sara said. "And, of course, one cousin was named Emil. He was very short, according to my mother, Helga."

"Emil Stoltzfus?" The deacon stood up and his voice got louder. "Emil Stoltzfus?"

Mary Beiler paused and came to stand beside the deacon. She was not smiling anymore, either.

"Is something wrong?" Sara said.

Mary Beiler and Deacon Schmidt looked at each other, and he started talking to her, very fast, in German. Then he turned and walked out of the room.

"Meidung," he muttered.

"I'm sorry," Mary Beiler said to them. "But I think you should leave."

"But I don't understand," Sara said. "What about our family reunion?"

"I'm sorry," Mary Beiler said again. "But Emil Stoltzfus is not someone we like to talk about. Do you know the German word *'Meidung?'* "

"It means shunned, someone who's shunned, doesn't it?" Sam said. "Is Emil Stoltzfus being shunned by the sect?"

"I'm afraid so," Mary Beiler said. "We don't see him. We don't talk about him. We aren't sure where he's gone. I'm sorry—I know this must be difficult for you since he's your cousin, but he did a very bad thing."

"What did he do?" Sam asked gently.

But Mary Beiler had turned and followed the deacon from the room.

The imposters from Wichita got up and walked out of the house. On the front porch a tall man who had followed them out stopped them. "I know you," he said.

"We're the Stoltzfuses," Sara said, pretending not to recognize John Brower.

"No, you aren't," Brower said. "You aren't even related to him. You came to our house with the professor. You've been looking for Stoltzfus, though. You probably want to find him for the same reason those other men did."

"I'm sorry. I don't know what you're talking about."

"Die Kugel." Brower stared hard, first at Sara, then at Sam. He turned and walked back into the house.

TWENTY-THREE

Calvesi skulked in the bushes, wearing a dark down parka and a black leather cap with two fake fur flaps that lightly covered his ears. The flaps concealed the ear buds of the stethoscope that Calvesi wore. From a distance he looked like Doogie Howser, M.D., on a ski vacation.

He scraped against sharp branches as he circled the house, putting the receiver of the stethoscope on different windows in an attempt to pick up transmissions from inside. Night and the relative emptiness of the countryside helped obscure the little man's movements. He moved through clumps of hibernating rhododendron until he got to the kitchen, which he could see brightly illuminated through the window. He squatted behind a shrub and reached up, holding the scope against the lower corner of a bottom windowpane.

A horrifying whistling noise filled his ears. Then the slightly muffled voice of a woman.

These things were more useful for eavesdropping than safecracking, a trade that Calvesi never could master because his ears were not sensitive enough to pick up the sounds of tumblers dropping. He listened in.

"What the hell are you whistling?" the voice (Sara's voice) said.

Jake was neck-deep in his refrigerator, cleaning it.

"Greetings," the professor said, emerging from under the cheese shelf and running a Lestoil-soaked hand through his hair. *The Barber of Seville?*"

"Sounds like 'Rock Lobster,' by the B-52s," Sara said.

"I thought it was 'Psycho Killer,' " Sam said.

"This is no time to bring up the Talking Heads, Sam," Sara said, shifting Baby from one hip to the other.

"You both must be tone-deaf."

They allowed as how the acoustics inside the refrigerator probably were distorting the notes and suggested that the problem would be solved as soon as Jake finished throwing away the rotted fruit that made his Tupperware containers swell unnaturally.

Mollified, he asked, "Having any luck tracking Emil Stoltzfus?"

"Not really," Sam said. "In fact, every time we get new information, it just confuses us more."

"Then you must not be fitting the pieces together logically," Jake said. He wiped his hands on a dish towel. He did not look up. If he had, he would have seen Sara rolling her eyes to the ceiling and silently mimicking his professorial mien.

"We know we're not doing something right," Sam said. "But if we knew what, we'd have solved the problem already and would be at home, in front of our computer where we belong, typing the final draft of the Eastern Pennsylvania issue of *The Thin Man*."

"Uh-huh." Jake tossed a brown-edged head of iceberg lettuce over his shoulder into the garbage can, picked up a wedge of cheddar and held it up to the light to look for mold.

"Hey, you're throwing this out?" Sam was rummaging through a wax-wrapped carton of baked goods. He took a tentative bite of a deep-fried chocolate doughnut. "Still moist."

Sara snatched it from his hand and tossed it on top of the lettuce. "All we know is we followed your advice," she said to Jake. "We went back to Stoltzfus's house yesterday to get the Bible. And now we're in worse shape than when we started, when we knew he was the dead body. Now we still know he's the dead body, but we don't know who all these live ones are who are wandering around."

Jake winced. "Sara, take a deep breath before you speak. Use that time to organize your thoughts."

"Jake, you can kneel here in front of your dirty refrigerator in torn jeans and act like you're going to flunk me for handing in a term paper with misspellings. Or you can help us figure this out. And then we'll go away and leave you alone, we promise," Sara said.

Jake decided to try tolerance.

"You went to Stoltzfus's house again," Jake said.

"We were looking for the Bible. For the family tree," Sam said. "And we found it."

"But just as we're getting ready to leave, these two creepy-looking guys drive up, so we lay low in the pantry," Sara said. "They come in. And they start to tear the place up, looking for something."

"And?" Jake was scraping something brittle and sticky from the shelf inside the door. It could have been syrup.

"You keep syrup in the refrigerator?" Sam asked.

"Weird." He reached into the fruit bin and pulled out an apple, polished it on his shirt before taking a bite.

"Whatever it was, they didn't find it. They saw that the Bible was missing and that seemed to discourage them, only I don't think it was the Bible they were looking for. We followed them to see what else we could find out," Sara continued. "To a motel in Blue Ball, where we find out they're from out of town."

Jake began reshelving the unspoiled perishables.

"That butter is rancid!" Sara shrieked. "I can smell it."

Jake and Sam ignored her.

"Then what happened?" Jake asked.

"Then this morning we went to the Beiler house, where you said the Bremmers were having their Sunday service," Sara said. "At first Deacon Schmidt was very nice. But when he heard we're related to Emil Stoltz—"

"You're not related to Stoltzfus," Jake said.

"We know that. You know that," Sara said. "But the deacon was confused. Anyway, when he heard Stoltzfus's name, he got this dark look on his face and clammed up. Then Mrs. Beiler came over, and they started talking in German. Waving their arms. Saying *meidung, meidung.* Shouting something about noodle pudding over and over. I mean, it was weird, these pacifistic people getting all hostile."

"Noodle pudding?" Jake asked.

Yeah, something about the Kugel."

Jake was staring at her.

"Jake? Jake?" Sam said. "Oh, Professor Fisher, your ice cream is melting all over the linoleum."

"Did you say Die Kugel?" Jake said in a low voice. "Die Kugel?"

They nodded.

"Incredible," Jake murmured, more to himself than to his visitors. He left the remaining perishables in the sink and went into the living room. They could hear him fishing for something in the bookshelves, shoving aside old copies of *Consumer Reports* and *The New England Journal of Medicine.* He came back carrying a dusty brown book that looked as if it had been published by a vanity press. In fact, it was a doctoral thesis titled 'Myths and Symbols of the Anabaptists."

They waited.

"Impossible." He flipped through a few pages. Stopped. Read a bit, then flipped deeper into the book and hummed like a computer.

"Ahhhh," Jake said at last. He cleared his throat, then read aloud:

"Of all the symbols one may observe in Amish and Mennonite life, none is more controversial—nor contradictory—than Die Kugel. Indeed, the vast majority of Anabaptist scholars have vigorously maintained that the story of the jewel-encrusted, eighteen-carat-gold orb is little more than myth. The Anabaptist religions, these same scholars argue, emphasize humility and leading a possession-free life; the concept of a golden calf, as it were, let alone the reality, would be unthinkable."

"Was this translated from some other language?" Sara asked.

"It's in thesis, Frenchie. This is how it's supposed to sound."

Jake continued reading:

"Yet the Amish and Mennonite religions are nothing if not sectarian. A recent study of the Kishacoquillas Valley in Mifflin County, Pennsylvania, for instance, revealed no fewer than twelve distinct Amish-related

groups, each with its own manner of dress and worship—"

"Ahem," Sara coughed politely. Jake looked up from the
book and glowered. She smiled.

"Die Kugel, a symbol of both The Glory of God and
God's Damnation, was first described in a journal
kept by Elizabeth King, an Englishwoman who emi-
grated to Lancaster County in 1767. In her journal
King referred to a golden orb "the size of God's right
eye and almost as bright" and a "ball of gold and
jeweled bounties from the earth" that gave hope to the
nine members of her sect during their torturous voy-
age across the Atlantic. King, whose husband, Freder-
ick, was deacon of the group, wrote that 'Die Kuggel
. . . (sic.) . . . is invested with all that was worldly and
moneywise in this, the Low Kingdom of God' and was
'an ease on the conscience of the Brethren who could
turn to it when they felt the need to acquire . . . and
that need would be dissolved and a contentment
would settle in.' "

"What the hell does that mean?" Sara asked.
"It means, Frenchie, that there was this big, expensive
ball that they all gathered around to touch whenever they
needed to quell an urge to go shopping at Sak's."
"Now I get it."
Jake continued:

"In yet another reference to the orb, Elizabeth King
described how it was made by her grandfather, Gustav, a German craftsman, in 1696, at the height of the
War of the Palatinate, when Louis XIV ordered his

armies to raze the Palatine. Hordes of starving peasants had been reduced to roaming the countryside, looking for food and goods to sustain them. The orb, she wrote, was made from all of the gold jewelry of the region, which was collected by one of the hordes and placed at the renowned craftsman's feet. The peasants asked Gustav King to melt down the gold and roll it into a large ball; they then presented him with scores of precious and semiprecious stones and had him hammer the gems into the orb. The peasants were so taken with King's skill that they asked him to hold onto the orb; when the time came, they said, use it as ransom to the French and save their lives.

"However, on a night when Gustav slept, 'well likkered and deep in his muttons,' a troop of French soldiers slipped into his village and set fire to it, slaughtering most of the residents. Gustav and his family barely escaped—with the orb. He was so grateful his life was spared that he converted to Anabaptism. 'He admired their simple manner of dress, and felt he looked good in black,' Elizabeth King wrote.

"Elizabeth King's journal, found in the library of an Amish home for the aged in 1965, provides the historian with the only record of the sect. According to King, it was Die Kugel which led to a tripartite split that destroyed the group; members were ultimately aligned with other districts in the Lancaster County area and, like a giant shell game, to this day it remains unknown which of the members, if any, held onto the mysterious—and possibly mythical—Kugel. An interesting footnote: It is well established that all cases of Ellis-van Creveld syndrome—a form of dwarfism whose victims often have six-fingered hands—are directly traceable to the 1767 crossing of Elizabeth King and her sect."

"Did I hear the word *dwarf* somewhere in the middle of that mush?" Sara asked.

They all sat quietly for a minute.

"I don't get it," Sara said.

"I am trying to be patient," Jake said. "The way I am patient with a student who raises her hand on the first day of the semester, during a particularly inspired bit of my lecture, and asks: Will we have to know this for the final?"

"Jake, will we have to know this for the final?" Sam asked. He picked another apple from the top shelf of the refrigerator.

"Most definitely. What I am trying to tell you is that Die Kugel, which learned religious historians have for years—for centuries actually—considered to be mere myth, may in fact be an actual object, a thing, something you could put your hands on. Something the Bremmers had their hands on, until one day when Mr. Emil Stoltzfus took it off their hands."

"Stole it?" Sam asked.

"It seems likely. In fact, it sounds like he was even shunned for his misdeed," Jake said. "And apparently, he disappeared. With Die Kugel."

"Does that thesis say how much a solid gold ball encrusted with jewels might be worth?" Sara asked. "Like, if it was being auctioned by Sotheby's or something?"

"Sara, you haven't been listening," Jake said. "Nobody even thought the thing existed. Scholars the world over have considered Die Kugel a myth, a legend. You can't very well appraise a legend."

"Seems like it must be pricey," Sara said. "Worth millions, probably."

"It's priceless—if it exists."

Sam spoke up. "Certainly worth enough to kill someone over."

Outside, Calvesi rubbed his hands together. This was getting better and better.

TWENTY-FOUR

Stan Smith was not used to leaving the womblike safety of his native Manhattan for the wilds of America. He did it so seldom that he was ill prepared for such foreign customs as strangers smiling at him on the streets and gas station attendants offering to check his oil. In fact, he drove a car so infrequently that he was not entirely sure where the oil was or why it needed to be checked or whether this was some kind of trick.

Smith did not consider himself untrusting. He was not a fellow particularly prone to suspicions. At home, on the Upper West Side, he was just as easygoing as the next guy. If, for instance, he was on line for twenty minutes at Zabar's, inching toward the cash register and clutching a half pound of andouille sausage integral to a jambalaya that Sam was concocting, and a woman in a fur coat suddenly shoved her way in front of him, Smith would not jump to the conclusion that she wanted to cut the line. No, he would consider the situation, realize that the pound of Nova she carried would suffer more from extended exposure to the elements (read: the overwarm air, tempered with the aromas of fresh-ground coffee and fresh-baked bread that is Zabar's) than the sausage he meant to purchase, and say nothing. In fact, he might silently congratulate the woman for her stalwart advocacy of sliced smoked salmon. But that was different; that was a typical situation that you might expect on any day. That was home. Out here, a hundred and fifty miles from the comforting honks and sirens of upper Broadway, things seemed too quiet. People were too polite. What were they trying to pull?

All in all, it had been a harrowing day, what with the unsettling encounter with Stavropoulos, and then the more unsettling encounter with the transmission of a rental car. Which still seemed to be grinding its gears in a distressing manner.

This was not at all how Smith liked to spend his Sundays, especially during football season, especially a season that had propelled the Giants into a playoff berth. On a playoff Sunday it was not easy to convince Smith to abandon the Coke-stained comfort of his bunchy gray couch (which had seemed so deceptively comfortable on the showroom floor at Conran's, its smooth upholstery supporting a discreet sign: $450) and the promise of Microwave popcorn at the half. It took a real emergency to compel a man like Smith—who had in the past been known actually to attend games in the subfreezing open-air stadium at the Meadowlands, where he once shed his ill-fitting shirt to reveal a bright blue GIANTS painted across his chest during a crucial contest against the Eagles—to turn off the TV and force his weekend self into a vertical position long enough to get dressed, much less to take a subway downtown to pick up a wheezing subcompact with murderous transmission problems.

And to convince a man like Smith to fold his luxury-sized body into that uninvitingly tiny driver's seat and to suppress his dual fears of tunnels and suburbia long enough to gain entry to the New Jersey Turnpike—well, that real emergency had to approach crisis proportions. Like the threat of nuclear attack. Or the rumor that the Coca-Cola Bottling Co. planned to suspend production of low-calorie beverages. Or the possibility that his best friends were in real trouble.

Smith turned sharply into a parking lot, shuddering when a car in the other lane honked loudly and swerved momentarily into the ditch at the side of the road. Maybe he should have used a blinker to signal his intentions to turn. Well, he would have been glad to, had he remembered that this car had blinkers. Did all cars have blinkers? Now that he thought about it, probably. Transmissions and blinkers. And oil, though God knows what for, since they supposedly run on gasoline. Another trick? The heartlands instilled paranoia.

Smith parked.

Sam and Sara were arguing over the ham croquettes. Or, more precisely, over whether the ham croquettes were simply a deep-fried version of the excellent ham salad they had just sampled.

"No, there's another taste, something elusive," Sam insisted. "The spicing is different."

"Sam, I picked it apart. I picked off the crust. Look at this croquette. No crust. In the nude it looks just like the ham salad. And tastes the same," Sara insisted. "Good, though."

"I think we might be judging the ham dishes too precipitously," Sam said. He pushed back his chair.

"More of that dried corn relish for me," Sara called after him as her husband sidled up to the painfully spotless and shiny aluminum counter that ran the length of the restaurant. On the counter, in individual trays, were dozens of dishes that deserved sampling: pan-fried chicken, buttery whipped potatoes, fruit pies, crispy shredded cabbage and lettuce. And ham croquettes.

While Sam ladled generous portions onto a plate still warm from the restaurant's overworked dishwasher, Sara made a halfhearted attempt to interest Baby in the wet and wadded bits of cheese bread that the infant had balled up on the highchair's tray.

"Mommy and Daddy like this restaurant," Sara told Baby. "Does Baby like the food, too? Should Mommy and Daddy remind their infant readers not to overlook the Play-Do possibilities of the homemade breads?"

Sam came back, sat down, and pulled out his notebook. But instead of jotting down his wife's more brilliant food observations, as was his habit on assignment, he wrote a heading across the top of the page, WHAT WE KNOW:

One, Stoltzfus is in financial trouble.

"Right? His farm is going under, according to those liens we turned up in the courthouse. So he's looking for some way to raise money, and raise it fast," he said.

"Correct," said Sara. "Two. He steals this very valuable treasure, this gold ball, from his congregation. That part makes sense."

"We're agreed so far," Sam said, scribbling. "He steals it. But he has to turn it into money somehow, unless the various mortgage companies would accept pieces of a jewel-encrusted orb."

"Three: Someone kills him. Why? To get the Kugel—which they probably didn't get," said Sara.

"How do you figure?"

"If the guy who killed him had gotten it, there would be no need to go to his house looking for it. That house was searched twice, from one end to the other," Sara said.

"Right," Sam said. "I'm sure Thomson and Otis didn't find what they came for."

"So are they the people who killed him?" Sara asked.

"Maybe. Or they work for whoever killed him. Maybe Thomson was the person he was supposed to sell the thing to in the first place. Who else would even know Stoltzfus had it in his possession?"

"How about the people he stole it from?" Sara asked. "All those people in his sect?"

"I just don't think murder is their style," Sam said. "Pacifistic people. Et cetera."

"Okay, so the goons are at his house after he's been killed, searching for Die Kugel. Why couldn't they find it?"

"Stoltzfus hid it," Sam said. "But why would he hide it in the first place?"

"Because he knew he was in danger?" Sara said. "Because he knew other people knew he had Die Kugel?"

"Right, right," said Sam. "But the thugs searched his house. We searched his house. Where else could the thing be?"

"Four: A dead end. That thing could be anywhere," Sara said. Her chin settled into her palms. "Where do you normally hide something? In a closet?"

"There aren't any in an Amish house."

"Under a bed?"

"His bed was too small to hide a toothpick."

"He could bury it," Sara said.

"The ground's frozen. Too difficult. Too risky if you think you're being followed."

172

"So he hides it . . . Sam . . . the receipt!"

"What receipt?" Sam crinkled his nose. "Oh, right." He fished around in one of the many pockets that hung from his parka. "Right, right, right. He hides it . . ."

"In a piece of furniture!" Sara yelled.

A woman carrying a tray supporting a bowl of soft ice cream and six plates of different pies swerved protectively as Sara flung out her arms. Sara looked for a second at the woman, then turned to the tattered receipt Sam was smoothing on the table.

"Let's see . . . a bunch of junk," he said. "Altogether, Bainey gave him only two hundred dollars. Let's see, table, footstool, chairs, clock—"

"Clock?" Sara said. "Didn't Jake Fisher say something about a clock once?"

"Yeah, you're right," Sam said. "When that windbag was gassing about what you can expect to find in an Amish house. He said Stoltzfus should have a clock—a tall, hand-carved clock would be something he gave to his fiancée before they got married."

"So why would he sell something with such sentimental value?"

"Unless he planned to get it back," Sam said. He was excited. "Unless he hid something of great value inside the clock where nobody could find it but him when the time was right. He sold the clock to Bainey with Die Kugel hidden inside. Better than a safe-deposit box. And he planned to buy it back when things cooled off. I'll bet you."

"You mean we have to go see that jerk Bainey again to get it back?" Sara asked.

"Tomorrow," Sam said. "Don't forget: His store is closed on Sunday."

"I can't wait," Sara said. "I'm too excited."

"Let's try to concentrate on our other problem, then,"

Sam said. "Making a living. If we don't do some real work, *The Thin Man* is not going to be ready to go out by deadline. And that could cause serious cash flow problems for a certain couple who have to pay the rent every month."

He flipped to a clean page in his notebook and wrote:

Both the ham salad and the ham croquettes are excellent renditions of traditional Pennsylvania Dutch fare. It is difficult to choose one over the other, although there is an elusive and sophisticated element to the spicing in the croquette not evident in the—

He broke off as his wife plucked his sleeve. "Sara, don't take it personally. Didn't I accept, verbatim, your poetic description of the pineapple fritters?"

"Sam, forget the ham for a minute. Look."

Sara gestured toward the entrance of the Shady Maple smorgasbord, where tourists in a long line were waiting their turn for a table and all they could eat. Amid the throng one man stood out. He emanated an air of sweaty uncomfortableness and urban suspicion the way Ivana Trump emanated eau de cologne.

"Smith!" Sam called. "Smith!"

"What are you doing here?" Sara asked their bulky friend as he ambled sheepishly up to their table.

"I thought you guys could use some advice," Smith said, pulling off his stained down jacket and draping it over the back of a chair. An empty Diet Coke can fell out of an inside pocket and onto the floor.

"How did you find us? Why are you even looking for us? My God, isn't it Sunday? Aren't the Jets playing?" Sam asked.

"The Giants." Smith valiantly tried to conceal a stricken look. "The Giants are playing. And I should be watching the game. Instead, however, I am forced to abandon the TV's remote control panel to the cockroaches, who probably are wasting the opportunity by watching the insect episode of *Wild Kingdom,* even as Phil Simms fades back to throw a once-in-a-career sixty-yard pass for a game-saving touchdown. But let's not talk about me."

"Ba-ba-ba-ba," Baby said.

"Listen, Smith, did you hear, she said, 'Smith,' " Sara said. "She said, 'How did Smith find Mommy and Daddy in Pennsylvania and why?' Did you hear her?"

"Tell her that Smith, fearing for the safety and freedom of Mommy and Daddy, tracked them down by driving to that weird used furniture store-slash-pigeon-barn that was mentioned in the newspaper articles last week. Tell her that the store was closed, so the smart lawyer looked up the owner's name in the phone book and drove to his house right down the road and asked him if he'd seen a couple of weirdos from the city. And tell her that Mr. Bainey said he recommended that those same two weirdos stop by his favorite restaurant, the Shady Maple, on their way out of town. The rest is serendipity, fate, the gods smiling, whatever.

"The important thing"—Smith paused to take a long pull from the plastic tumbler of Diet Coke that Sam had just put down in front of him—"is that I am here. I am here in time to save you, I hope, from the kind of Hitchcockian mixup that could land you in jail for a very long time."

"This is not like you, Smith," Sam said. "Not like you at all. What's got you so spooked?"

It had started that morning, when Smith, facing a long pleasurable day of football, had been nagged by a guilty feeling that he had been too tough on Detective Sergeant Evelyn Graber. He had placed a perfectly perfunctory call to the precinct, knowing full well that she worked most Sundays, planning to mollify her and mouth empty pledges to cooperate.

But instead of Graber, a very anxious Stavropoulos had picked up the phone. This in itself was unheard of. Stavropoulos was no more likely to be at his desk on a Sunday morning than Smith was to be fumbling for change at Exit 7 of the New Jersey Turnpike. But with Graber out of town—headed to Pennsylvania to apprehend Smith's own clients, in fact—the work did tend to pile up. Smith blew up. Smith shouted into the phone. Smith demanded an explanation. Nervously Stavropoulos had told all, even repeating the text of the anonymous letter and quoting from the case file about the discovery of Calvesi's ID bracelet in the open doorway of Sam and Sara's apartment.

"Open doorway? Back up," Sam said, clearly remembering the moment when he had turned the key in the lock, the sound the dead bolt had made when it engaged, the way his hand had closed on the cool doorknob to jiggle it just in case.

"Calvesi's ID bracelet? That's impossible," Sara said. "How could his bracelet be in our apartment, unless he was in our apartment?"

"Or unless it was planted there," Sam said.

"My God," Sara said.

"I know it all sounds ludicrous," Smith said. "But that makes it worse, if you ask me. There's no reasonable explanation for any of this—not the anonymous note, not Calvesi's disappearance, not the ID bracelet. And certainly not for the body you found in the first place. There is a distressing pattern of coincidence building up here."

"Distressing? I'd say it's a little more than distressing," Sam said. "And you don't have to be paranoid to see it's a little more than coincidence."

"In any case, an ugly situation is materializing. Graber is looking for you to arrest you for a murder. We can't explain that away," Smith said. "We've got to figure some way out of this. Are you guys still convinced that the corpse in your chest was the body of that farmer, that Stuckpuss guy? We can go to the cops here and tell them."

"Stoltzfus," Sam said. "Yeah, we think he's the dead guy, and we even think we know why he was killed, and we think we may have a way to find his murderer."

"We think we found the guy who sold us the chest," Sara added.

"No way. Enough already. This is the end of your amateur sleuthing," Smith said. "You have no business investigating—in fact your muddling may be what's getting you mixed deeper. I want you to come with me right now, or as soon as Baby's face is chiseled clean of bread crust, to the police to get this settled."

"Smith, if we do that, we'll be arrested," Sam said. "You're the one who told us Graber has a warrant."

"But if you don't do that, you'll be arrested anyway," Smith said. "And if you give them a reasonable explanation, we should be able to clear this up. I know how to deal with cops. I spent years attending the most expensive schools in the country for the express purpose of learning how to intimidate cops."

"Okay, we'll go with you," Sam said. "Tomorrow morning. Right after we ask Mr. Bainey about this furniture receipt."

TWENTY-FIVE

On the last morning of his life, Marlin Bainey stood behind the counter, wearing a big bandage on his right thumb that made it awkward for him to count the bills in the old cash register. Little notes were taped to the side: "No Checks," "No Credit," "No Layaway."

"Layaway?" Sara asked. 'Who would want to put a bunch of moldy old books on layaway? If you're going to buy something like that, you'd want to get them home right away, while the print is still readable."

Tufts of wild hair punctuated Bainey's exasperation. He snorted.

"That was a joke, Mr. Bainey," Sara said.

"You again."

"Sorry to bother you on such a busy day." There were no

other customers in the barn, unless you counted a couple of pigeons who were lazily inspecting a pile of yellowing Harlequin romances.

"No bother, really, at this point." Bainey sounded resigned. "I hear so much about you two that I'm starting to feel like you're family."

"What do you mean?" Sam said.

"Seems a day doesn't go by that I don't get badgered to talk about you two. First it was the Lancaster cops. Then you show up. The cops again. Now you again. Wouldn't mind so much if somebody would buy something once in a while."

"What a coincidence," Sara said. "We came with cash."

Bainey was suddenly interested.

"We'd like to buy a clock, a big clock."

"You want to buy a clock? An expensive clock?" Bainey asked slowly, as if Sara had just suggested sexual intercourse.

"Not necessarily expensive," Sam said hastily. "But we are looking for a clock."

"I got a bunch. Grandfathers, mantel clocks, wristwatches."

"We want to buy a specific clock, a clock you recently acquired. The clock that Emil Stoltzfus sold you."

"Who?"

"Emil Stoltzfus. A farmer who lives off Elam Road. Alone. Short guy. Sold you some furniture earlier this month. Here's the receipt." Sam proffered the slip of paper.

"Yeah, I remember," said Bainey after a moment. "Can't sell you that clock, though."

"Why not?" asked Sara.

"I unloaded it on Whitey Dietrich. Wasn't worth much."

'Whitey Dietrich?"

"Runs an auction house, has auctions year 'round. Good tourist attraction. He likes to pick through my stuff for 'authentic' Pennsylvania Dutch furniture. Got that clock and some other stuff right after I bought it from that Stoltzfus feller. All that stuff probably goes up on the block this afternoon."

Sam and Sara looked at each other, aware that the image of Dietrich's auction catalog on the dashboard of a certain rental car was flashing through both their minds simultaneously. "One, two, three, you owe me a Coke," Sara whispered, knocking Sam's arm ten times.

"Uh, just a little game we play," Sam told Bainey. "Private joke."

"Mr. Bainey, you wouldn't happen to know of a Merle Otis, would you?" Sara asked.

"Twenty questions again, eh?" Bainey sighed. Sara smiled. "No, I do not know a Mr. Merle Otis," he said.

"One more and that's it, I swear," Sara said, holding up her hand. She and Sam looked hard at Bainey. "Jeffrey Thomson—a guy with real, real pale skin?"

"Course I know Jeff," said Bainey. "Just saw him the other day. He was in here, looking for some new merchandise. Goes through my stuff pretty often."

"He does?" Sam asked.

"Yup. He worked for me summers as a kid. Only part-timer I ever trusted with a key to the place. I taught him everything he knows about the salvage business. Of course, he don't call it that. He's an antiques dealer now. Still the salvage business, but he charges more. Been running his own outfit for a good five years. Lives in Pittsburgh, I think. Oh, yeah, yeah. That other feller you mentioned? He's got a helper, Merle. That's right. How do you know Jeff?"

"A friend told us to look him up. She said he had quite an interesting collection of Mission furniture," Sara said.

"Well that's something I don't know about. Never seems to be looking for that stuff when he comes in here. And I haven't seen his shop ever. Mission furniture, huh? Must be a lot of money in it. *Ay, ya-ee, ya-eeee.*" Bainey shook his head and smiled. "That Jeff has a good head on his shoulders."

Five minutes later, as Sam and Sara drove off, another customer pulled into the dirt road, someone Bainey would remember as Detective Oudinot and a man Sam and Sara would greet as Dominic Calvesi. A man unlikely, in either incarnation, to buy junk furniture; Calvesi was allergic to dust, as well as to pig dander.

"You promised, you gave your word, you said no crossies," Smith whined. "Just let us make one futile trip to a junk store and then we swear on the head of our infant that we'll drive immediately to the police station and come clean, you said."

"I think you're twisting our words, Smith," Sam said. "What's a little detour to an auction?"

"All out of context," Sara said. "You should have been a journalist. You have a real flair for the dramatic."

The five of them—Baby had insisted on bringing along Pengie—were driving not toward Lancaster police headquarters, but in the opposite direction, in fact, toward Dietrich's Auction House.

"I admire your tenacity, really I do." Smith had abandoned whining for outright lies. "It shows strength of character. But I think the police are much better suited to these sorts of forays. In writing the Constitution, our forefathers considered this circumstance, and decided that instead of putting nice law-abiding civilians to the inconvenience of solving their own crimes, it would save everybody time and effort to create cops. Codicil 4B of some amendment: Cops, not food critics, should go to auctions to buy stolen goods. That's why we pay taxes."

"He's babbling," Sam said to Sara.

"Are you aware that you're babbling?" Sara asked Smith. She turned up the radio, pointedly signaling a great interest in the local weather forecast: "Light drizzle this afternoon to freeze into—we interrupt this forecast with a news bulletin," the announcer said.

"News? Out here? Unusual," Sam said.

"Cute," Sara said.

The announcer went on. "Police are reporting the discovery of the body of a forty-eight-year-old local farmer, who was found an hour ago on his property. The authorities suspect foul play in the shooting death of Marlin Bainey—"

"Bainey? What? BAINEY?" Sara said.

". . . a single gunshot wound to his head. Pending further investigation, police say they have no apparent suspects. But after interviewing nearby neighbors, police say they are seeking a late-model, dark green van with out-of-state plates, seen leaving Bainey's driveway earlier this morning. In other news, the county's elementary-school lunch menus for the week will feature pizza on Monday . . ."

"My God," Sam said. "They're looking for us."

He switched off the radio, and amazed silence filled the vehicle. Almost by itself, the car nosed off the road into a parking lot behind an insurance agent's office.

"Bainey dead?" Sara said. "We just saw him, not an hour ago."

Smith looked very pale.

"He wasn't such a bad guy, Bainey," Sara said. "Sam, Sam, Sam. What are we going to do?"

"Someone is trying to set us up," Sam said.

"Very successfully," Smith said.

"Jesus, we really are going to go to jail," Sam said. "It does look like we killed some midget and then offed Bainey to shut him up before he could testify that we never went to his store last Sunday."

Smith had no time for such reflection. His was the mind of a trained attorney, already focusing on the big ethical and moral question: How much bail could he raise? Aloud, he said, "My argument for turning yourselves in is starting to sound less compelling, even to me."

His clients stared at him in shock. "Should we flee to Rio?" Sara snapped. "Is that your latest advice?"

"Calm down, Sara," Sam said.

"So what do *you* suggest *we* do?" Smith said.

"Well, there's no way to prove that we've heard the news of Bainey's death yet," she said slowly. "And if we don't know he's dead, we can't know we're suspects. So I would think we would just continue on to the auction and try to buy the Kugel."

"Oh, right," Smith said. "Maybe get into a bidding war with Graber. Don't you think Manhattan's Finest is minutes away from swooping down on two murderous food critics?"

"Possible. Listen: I have an idea," Sara said. "When Thomson sees us at the auction, he'll recognize us—"

"Oh, great," Smith said.

". . . from when he sold us the corpse," Sara said. "He'll know we figured it out. So if we bid on something, he'll figure it's because we know Die Kugel is inside. All we have to do is buy the furniture. And then Thomson will come to us."

"With guns and brass knuckles and meat cleavers," Smith said. "With beheading devices and hand-removal tools. How is that a plan?"

"Don't be obtuse," Sara said. "That's where you come in. You'll be watching, discreetly, if possible, and when Thomson approaches us, *bam,* you call the cops."

"Cops arrive, we turn over the suspect and the evidence," Sam said. "End of case."

"Oy," said Smith. Sam turned on his blinker and pulled back out into traffic, the idea registering even as his mind traveled elsewhere, back to the middle of a muddy pigpen, where a red-faced man in torn overalls was standing in hip boots, banging on a hut with a stick and crooning, "Here, Scarlett, come on out, girl, we have company. Come on, girl, they won't hurt you. They're friends."

Graber did not own hip boots. Rarely would a New York City police detective slog through wet mud and long, matted weeds to reach the scene of a homicide, so Graber's usually well-equipped travel bag had failed her. The coffee thermos and yellow highlighters she carried did nothing to protect her shoes and ankles and legs from becoming encrusted out here in this not-quite-frozen pigpen. Noonan, who had pulled the requisite pair of rubber boots from his trunk, noticed that she made squishy noises as she shifted from foot to foot, staring down at Bainey's crumpled body.

What was left of Bainey, aside from the big chunks of brain and ears and bloody bone that had sprayed the ground with a fine pink mist in a radius of several feet, was lying face down in the mud. He had fallen on top of some magazine or pamphlet he apparently had been clutching; Graber could see the corner of it peeking out from under his torso: D-I-E-T-R-, she read. A clue, perhaps, although as far as Graber was concerned, the only puzzle left to solve was whether the trigger actually had been pulled by Sam or by Sara.

"My money's on the wife," she said to Noonan, who was attempting to extricate the Dietrich's Auction catalog from the corpse.

"Oh, yeah? How's that?" he asked.

"Call it a hunch."

"That ought to make interesting testimony in court."

A subtonic snort rumbled from the pig's hut. Graber looked up in disgust.

"Nope," Noonan said. "Nope, it just doesn't add up. Here is the store owner, dead. Here are the neighbors' reports, saying that an out-of-state vehicle carrying a man and a woman was seen pulling away from the barn less than an hour before a gunshot makes them call police. And here is a too-obvious motive: murderers trying to cover their tracks by closing permanently the big mouth of a witness. All very neat. Too neat, really."

"Life, or death for that matter, is often neat, Lieutenant," Graber said. "Evidence points us to a neat solution: the food critics. They're both looking at life in the hoosegow."

"If it looks too good to be true, it probably is. That's my mot-to." A frown creased Noonan's already weathered face.

He knelt down and, using the tips of his thumb and index fingers to form a pincer, retrieved a pink wad from the ground by Graber's feet. "Bainey chew gum, I wonder?" he asked.

"I must call my office," Graber said. "Immediately."

"May be a phone in the barn," Noonan called over his shoulder as he carried the pink wad of physical evidence over to the team from the county crime lab. "Let's analyze the saliva on this one," he said. He dropped the gum into a clear plastic bag and handed it to them to label.

A small circle of officialdom had formed: the medical examiner, a photographer, an investigator from the district attorney's office, and the two police officers who had been first to respond to the report that Mrs. Smitty Herzog from down the road had heard a loud, sort of a backfire of a noise while she had been sweeping off her back stoop. She wouldn't have thought twice about it, really, but for the fact that the usually complacent crows in the tree behind the garage had startled, flown from their branches, and circled, chattering in the air for a minute before they settled down again.

Later the crows had flown over to Bainey's for a closer look, arriving well before the police and perching on Scarlett's hut to get a good view of the corpse. The pig had so far refused to emerge from her quarters, reluctant to confront either the crowd of strangers tromping through her turf or the fallen shape of her owner. It was too bad, really, because if the police had been as persistent in interviewing her as they had been in setting up an official crime scene—a rarely used roll of yellow tape screaming Do Not Cross had been unwound and draped across the barbed-wire fence, and bright red-and-blue lights were blinking on top of the three police cars parked a few dozen yards away—they would have learned why Bainey had abandoned the comparative warmth of his space-heated barn for the icy isolation of the open field.

They would have learned that Bainey, grumbling in a good-natured way, had just finished repeating his conversation with Sara and Sam to Detective Oudinot, had just explained that for some reason those rude out-of-towners were headed to Whitey Dietrich's to buy up some furniture. The police would have known that Oudinot had nodded, grateful, and then suggested that Bainey go over things one more time—the detective particularly wanted the store owner to retrace the sequence of events of the first visit the New Yorkers had paid him. "Well, I showed them my best pig," Bainey had said. "I thought their kid would enjoy meeting Scarlett. So we went outside—here, I'll show you—"

But none of the police officers standing out in the mud, not even Noonan, remembered the pig's presence. No one offered her the midmorning snack of table scraps she was fond of: wilted carrot tops or mashed potatoes or apple peel or a bone with some meat left to lick clean.

So Scarlett stayed inside, in the dark, where no one bothered to search.

TWENTY-SIX

There was a long table just inside the door, a table like the ones folded up in the basements of elementary schools and dusted off when the PTA has a bake sale. Behind it sat a white-haired woman with a list. She looked like somebody's mom, the mom who had baked the butterscotch congo bars.

"Name?" she asked pleasantly.

"Sam Popkin and Sara Amstel," Sara said a little loudly. Smith winced and skulked miserably nearby, holding Baby, who strained, arms outstretched, in an apparent imitation of a medieval religious statue.

"Number 112," the registrar said, checking off a line on her list. "Do you need a catalog? No? That'll be ten dollars, then, for registration."

"I'm just glad this isn't the tourist season," said Sam. He

removed a bill from his pocket, unfolded it, uncrinkled it, and passed it over. The woman handed them a little sign with "112" lettered on it in black Magic Marker. They stepped around the table and into a room filled with rows of chairs upholstered in red vinyl. A multicolored banner with the words "Dietrich's Auction House" was at the front of the room, drooping from the rafters.

The place smelled of furniture wax and mold, an odd combination. It also smelled of . . . "Chicken noodle soup?" said Sam.

Chicken noodle soup, with homemade noodles, as it turned out, was for sale at a small concession stand near the entrance that also specialized in boiled hot dogs, steamed cheeseburgers, and a variety of canned soft drinks.

"We'd better try the soup," he said. "Just in case." He bought a small Styrofoam bowl of soup for a dollar fifty and contentedly sipped as Sara prowled the room.

Potential bidders shuffled, single file, around the perimeter of the room where the various lots were displayed. Little knots of people formed in front of the tables that held the more desirable objects—the Louis Comfort Tiffany leaded glass lampshade, the set of colonial pewter mugs and spoons, a genuine farmhouse pine kitchen table—and then thinned out again to a respectful single file, like mourners visiting a national hero lying in state in Red Square.

The bidders could be divided into roughly two groups, Sam decided: dealers, and dealers trying not to look like dealers. A tough crowd, he thought, watching a bespectacled man lick the tip of his pencil, jot a cryptic note in the margin of his catalog, and then hold up the book tò compare a photo of a spindle-backed rocker with the chair that sat on a riser in the corner of the room.

"Clock ahoy." Sara zipped off through the crowd, agilely avoiding the umbrella someone had leaned, point up, against a chair, and maneuvering around a collapsible stroller to reach the other side of the room.

Sam huffed up. "How do we know this is the one?" He anxiously flipped through the catalog, looking for photos of clocks, looking for the photo of this one clock, looking for some speck of information that would make this scheme seem less like a harebrained scavenger hunt.

The tall wooden clock had been elaborately carved, its imperfections and uneven gouges clearly less important than the painstakingly involved patterns of vines and hearts that covered it from foot to face. Lot 317, said the little white card leaning up against the clock. Lot 318, just to the right, was a low footstool and a set of four chairs. Lot 316, just to the left, was a much-used maple coffee table, one leg shorter than the other three, tenuously balancing a big redware bowl full of fruit.

"I bet all this stuff—these three lots—are from Stoltzfus, via Bainey," Sara said. "All this stuff was itemized on the receipt."

Sam moved close enough to run his finger over the ridge of the oak grain. The clock had a little wooden door cut into its side, a compartment that held the works, an intricate assemblage of well-oiled springs and levers and gears and—

"Die Kugel." Sam took mental measurements of the compartment. "I bet it's in there."

Sara consulted the catalog. "Lot 317. We have a long wait."

They threaded their way through the bidders, back across the room to where Baby and Smith sat, scanning the crowd for police.

"Let's change seats," Sam said. "We should sit in the back, so we can see everyone else who comes in."

People carrying little numbered signs were spilling down

the aisle, throwing overcoats across chair backs, staking out territory.

"I'm nearsighted," Sara whined.

"We aren't at a movie," Sam said, clearly a reference to that time she had made him sit in the front row at *The Dead* at the 62nd Street Theater. He had to sit staring directly up into Angelica Huston's strongly corded, six-foot-high neck for an hour and a half. She was an attractive woman, but please.

"Let's compromise." The last time they "compromised," Sara thought, she had to choke her way through *Dead Ringers* while pregnant (she had made involuntary gagging noises during the display of gynecological instruments for use on mutant women, but then the first trimester had been a time of intense gagging upon exposure to nearly everything, from dog shit on the sidewalk to cat food crusted on a saucer).

Smith settled it, standing up and moving to the side of the showroom, to seats that afforded a decent view of the auction, as well as of the main entrances.

"We should have just gone to the cops," Smith said. Baby had discovered Smith's nose and was googling with glee as she jammed a finger into his nostril. It cracked her up.

"Smith, we've been over this. And over this."

"I know, I know. I just feel uneasy about this whole scene," the attorney said. "It's starting to get a little farcical."

"You mean just because we bought a chest that had been stuffed with the headless, handless corpse of a midget whose house we subsequently broke into—twice—and we're now being hunted by people called Squidly and Fedora, who apparently killed the midget, and the vicious Graber who thinks we're the perps? And we're hot on the trail of a priceless antique that's as legendary as King Arthur's sword?"

"Ouch," Smith said, jerking his nose.

"Yeeeee," said Baby.

"You know," Smith said, kerplopping Baby's index finger out of his nose, "when you put it that way, it does all kind of seem logical, after all."

"The kind of stuff that happens all the time," Sara said.

"My point precisely. Look"—she pointed to the PTA table— "enter the cutthroats . . . don't turn around."

Sam turned around.

"Sam. I said don't." She pulled him into an eyeball-to-eyeball conference. "It's them."

"Them?" said Smith. "I need a Diet Coke. Where's the Diet Coke? Did you see a machine? A snack bar?"

Them were walking down the aisle, looking for seats to settle in. Thomson led the way, his eyes darting over the crowd. Merle Otis, who had seen one too many movie versions of John Dillinger's life, trailed, watching his boss's back and keeping one hand under his jacket.

Thomson and his minion quietly settled in two aisle seats, one row behind Sam, Sara, Smith, and Baby.

Sara stole a quick glance at the Evil Ones and gulped. The men were openly staring—Thomson even smiled a smile of recognition, his pale-lipped mouth spreading to expose yellowed teeth.

He was wearing a cheap-looking, ill-fitting silver-gray suit, and a polyester tie that featured brown, blue, and green stripes beneath silver sprinkles.

In truth, the tie was a lot less scarier than he was. Had Sara been able to watch, she would have seen Thomson pull a razor-sharp strip of metal from his pocket (it was a tin clasp, used to hold loose-leaf papers in court briefs.) Absentmindedly he dug into the gap between two lower front teeth that were rotting. It was a pleasant pain. Thomson hated going to dentists. Having one's teeth drilled was so . . . personal, he thought, flicking the metal strip suddenly.

"Excuse me," he said to Otis. The slip caused a fleck of plaque to splatter on Otis's sleeve.

"It's okay," Otis said, not looking up from his magazine. It really wasn't okay, not that he was going to say anything, thank you very much. Better to tolerate the boss's bizarre affectations than suffer his wrath, he thought. He perused a copy of *Penthouse* which he had disinterred from inside his molting overcoat, and turned to a lovely photographic essay that featured women with pubic hair shaved like shrubbery. Human topiary.

"My, they look jumpy," Sara said. "Of course, so does Stanley."

"This is not a good idea," said Smith. "Is that a cop?"

"It's a security guard, Stanley."

Watery eyes bored into their backs.

In the front of the room, two men came out from behind a musty velvet curtain, stepping up onto a makeshift wooden platform by the rostrum.

"Lot 7," the auctioneer called. "Lot 7." His assistant handed him a hatrack made of elaborately splayed moose antlers. "Do I hear fifty?"

Sam longed in his more private moments for an Adirondacks camp where he could stalk around with a walking stick, affecting a Teddy Roosevelt monocle. Sara squirmed and glanced at Squidly.

"He winked at me, darling."

"That's nice." Sam was thinking about the antlers.

Thomson and Otis stood up noisily and walked off in the direction of the refreshments.

"Do I hear thirty-five dollars?" the auctioneer said. "Fine rack here, folks. Beautify the den or study. Thirty dollars to start this auction off today."

Sara's hand clamped down on Sam's wrist, quick enough to trap a housefly but barely fast enough to stop him from waving their numbered sign in the air.

"Are you nuts?" she asked. "Moose antlers? Snap out of it."

"I could display my fez."

"Your fez is already displayed, on the mantel."

"I could display my fez in the entryway."

"We don't have an entryway. We live in Manhattan. We store our good china under the bed next to our camping equipment. We barely have a living room. Entryway." Sara rolled her eyes.

They stiffened. Amid the bickering, two big hairy hands had snuck up behind them, one clamping down on Sara's left shoulder, the other on Sam's right.

Luckily, the scary hands were attached to scrawny professorial arms.

"Jake," Sam said. "Molly. So good to see you."

"Quite a crowd," Jake said. "You two certainly are nervous. Keep this up and you'll knock over your chairs."

Sara remembered her manners. "Jake, Molly, this is Stan Smith. Our attorney."

Jake looked puzzled. "Lawyer?"

"How do you do?" The professional Smith smoothly shook hands with the Fishers. "I've heard so much about you both."

"We didn't know you were bringing a lawyer," Molly said.

"Neither did we," Sam said. "Smith—"

"Actually, I was just passing by," Smith said. "On my way to a hot-tub resort in the Poconos. And thought I'd stop in to see my old buddies."

Sam and Sara smiled stupidly and nodded.

Jake and Molly were still confused. But they settled, with puzzled expressions, into the chairs that were still warm from the sweaty bodies of Thomson and sidekick. Sara stood up and looked around. Neither Thomson nor Otis was anywhere to be seen. This made her more anxious than if they had been seated right behind them, glowering. This was not good.

The auction proceeded at a fairly brisk pace, for an auction. An hour went by. Then two. Sam and Sara ticked off the items that had been sold from a buyers' list that came with the catalog.

"No Thomson," Sara said.

Sam shrugged.

Finally, from behind the curtain the auctioneer's assistant wheeled out a dolly bearing a big clock. "Do I hear ten dollars?"

Sam held up their number.

"Ten, do I hear twenty, twenty, fifteen, twelve and a half?"

A man in a hat held up his number.

"Fifteen. Do I hear—twenty, I have twenty, I have twenty-five."

The man in the hat looked uncertain.

"Twenty-five, twenty-five," the auctioneer sang. "Twenty-five. Sold to number 112."

Sam and Sara stood up, nodded pleasantly to Molly and Jake, and walked over to the table to pay for their purchase. Then they went outside and waited for the auction house's workers to wheel it out to their car.

They didn't see Thomson and Otis. But from hiding places slouched behind the wheel of a rain-slicked pickup truck, Thomson and Otis definitely saw them.

TWENTY-SEVEN

"I hate winter." A freezing drizzle was soaking them and, although it was barely midafternoon, the sky, which had started the day gray, was dark and mottled, ready to throw up. Sam, hunched in his parka, stood next to the Rover, blowing fake smoke rings in the frosty air. He glanced alternately toward the auction house's back door and over his shoulder at the cars parked in straggly rows on the gravel lot.

"They don't set much store by asphalt in this state, do they?" Sara kicked a pebble into a dirty, half-frozen puddle. "Mud and gravel. Everywhere we go in Pennsylvania. Like all these roads and parking lots are just an afterthought. Weird."

" 'Rural' is a better word, Dutch."

"No, I mean weird that Thomson and his punk haven't shown up."

"Yeah, I expected them to pop right out once we got outside," Sara said.

But the only people in sight were a couple of young boys, wheeling the clock out the back door of the auction house, and Smith, who stepped from the showroom into a puddle.

"Now what?" Sam waved across the parking lot, beckoning to Smith, who was picking his way over icy patches, Baby in his arms. "I thought for sure we'd flush them."

"So much for melodrama," Sara said.

"Looks like it didn't work." Smith sounded tired. His feet were wet. His nose was sore. And the empty parking lot definitely made him nervous.

"Where do you want it?" The boys with the clock wore heavy work gloves. Smith thrust his own chapped hands into the pockets of his thin jacket. There was a hole in one of the pockets. How was it possible for wind to whip around like that under somebody's coat?

The workers wrapped the clock in a heavy tarp and lifted it gently off the dolly. They maneuvered it, horizontally, onto the roof rack of the Rover.

"Next stop, cops," Smith said. He watched the workmen begin to lash the clock to the rack. "If this is going to take a while, I'm going back in for a Diet Coke. And to call my office."

He handed Baby to Sara and made his way back across the icy parking lot, swearing softly under his breath every time he slipped and had to grab on to the cold metal fender of a vehicle.

"Thanks." Sam handed each of the boys a five-dollar bill. The young men looked at the bills like they'd never seen money before. "Jeez, thanks!" one of them said. "Yeah!" said the other, too surprised to think of anything else to say.

Sam hardly noticed. He took Baby from Sara and leaned

inside the back seat to initiate the complex and harrowing process of strapping her into the car seat.

Sara, toeing a second pebble and aiming it toward a thin sheet of ice on top of a nearby puddle, didn't notice Smith disappear inside the auction house, either. She didn't see the two workers go back in through the back door and slam it shut.

But she did see, when she looked up, the cold shark snout of a .9 millimeter pistol pointed at her.

"Sam."

Sam looked over his shoulder and saw his wife flanked by Thomson and Otis. A lot of guns seemed to be aimed at Sara's head.

"All of a sudden I feel like Bugs Bunny," she said.

"Give me the keys, Wu-wuh-wuh-wabbit," Thomson said to her. She looked at Sam, who had the keys. Sam slouched toward Thomson. "No, don't come any nearer. Toss them here." Sam thrust his left hand first into one of his many parka pockets, one whose zipper curved around his right side like a scar.

"Uh, uh, slowly there," said Thomson. Sam cautiously removed his hand—it was empty—and searched the right hip pocket. Nothing. He checked the smaller pouch under the hip pocket. He colored, and began searching the pockets on the left side of the coat. He frisked himself briefly, then plunged his hand into the lower, middle pocket, the one with the Velcro clasp and plastic zipper. A slight metallic jingle indicated success.

Thomson caught the keys and handed them to Otis. "Get it off the roof," he said. "Get the truck," he told Otis.

"You could have bid on it," Sara said. "We only paid twenty-five dollars."

"Button it," Thomson said. "You two have made enough trouble in the past week."

"We made trouble for you?" Sam said. "You're the one who sold us a dead body in a chest. We gave you fifty dollars. I wouldn't call that trouble. I'd call finding a corpse in the middle of your living room trouble."

Thomson allowed himself a thin smile. "Be glad it didn't leak in your Range Rover."

"What I don't understand is why you killed Emil Stoltzfus and put his body in that chest in Bainey's store, Jeff Thomson," Sam said.

"You know my name? How clever you are," Thomson said. "Why did I kill Stoltzfus? I never met the man. Otis killed him, sort of at my direction."

"You told your henchman to kill him?" Sara asked.

"No, no, dear wabbit. Get your facts straight. I told my . . . assistant to . . . persuade him. I needed some information."

"What about?"

"About why the little old man was trying to double-cross me and steal thousands and thousands of my hard-earned dollars." Thomson paused. "What a pretty heirloom." He fingered a string of amber beads around Sara's throat, pulling gently. "A choker?"

"Leave her alone," Sam said.

Thomson, holding the necklace taut, pressed the cold gun into Sara's temple. "Hope I don't leave a welt, dear." Then he nodded toward Otis, who slammed his fist into Sam's stomach.

Sam doubled over. He gagged and then retched.

Thomson seemed not to notice. "I guess this is what I get for doing business with someone I don't know. My mistake was in trusting a middleman—who vouched for Mr. Stoltzfus's sincerity and dire need for cash. So when I learned about the availability of a certain very valuable artifact that I'd been trying to find for years, I was more than happy to send him a deposit. A very generous deposit."

"Die Kugel." Sam choked. He was trying very hard to stand upright.

"Finding something that exotic would catapult you from being a two-bit junk dealer into the big time, wouldn't it?" Sara said. *"Nightline, People* magazine. You'd be famous." Thomson dropped his head pensively.

"Die Kugel would make a nice cover photo for *Newsweek*. All those precious jewels. All that gold," she said.

"It is undoubtedly very lovely," Thomson allowed.

"You haven't seen it?" Sam said.

"That pleasure awaits me," Thomson said. "Although I do consider myself to be its rightful owner already, having put down a hundred-and-fifty-thousand-dollar deposit, ten percent, pending delivery. The problem was, after I turned over the cash, there was no delivery."

"You killed a man for the price of a one-bedroom apartment?" asked Sara.

"Not even in a good neighborhood," added Sam. Sara was relieved to see that the shocked red flush was fading from his face.

"You stupid fools," Thomson hissed. He unclenched Sara's necklace and stepped back. "Don't you know how much Die Kugel is worth? Don't you know that I could turn around tomorrow and sell it for ten million, fifteen million, whatever price I might fancy?"

"All right, it's a duplex, with a park view, concierge, private garage—and a small house in Southampton," Sam said to Sara.

"Now I get it," Sara said.

"When I sent my assistant to find out why there was no delivery, Stoltzfus said he was having difficulty getting the orb. Merle used his unique powers of persuasion on the little man and convinced him to be a bit more forthcoming. Alas, he admitted that he did, in fact, have the object. But he had reappraised it and decided that it could fetch a higher price— elsewhere."

"Another buyer?" asked Sara.

"It would appear so," Thomson said.

A dented blue Chevy pickup pulled alongside them, its exhaust pipe ominously pooting smelly white fumes.

"Merle continued to . . . persuade the nasty little dwarf to reveal its whereabouts. He admitted to having hidden it in a piece of furniture, the little sneak. A piece of furniture which he sold to Bainey as part of a batch of household furnishings. He said he really couldn't remember which piece. So Merle took him down to Farm Salvage to refresh his tiny memory."

Stoltzfus, not a bold man even in his younger days, had been so frightened during the ride from his ransacked farm-house to the salvage barn that he had blacked out briefly. "Merle woke him up," Thomson said. "A little trick he has. I don't know that we need to repeat it in front of the lady—" He leered at Sara, who was trying desperately not to rub the bruised area on her neck.

"Not a pink belly?" Sara whispered, stricken.

Thomson said nothing.

"Indian rope burns? A wedgie? . . . You sick, sick bastards," she said.

Otis smirked.

"Unfortunately, soon after arriving at Farm Salvage, the little dwarf's heart just went boom. It must have been all the . . . excitement." Thomson affected a sad sigh.

"Alas," Thomson continued, "he never told us what piece of furniture held the goodies. And that caused some anxiety. We had to get rid of any identifiable dwarf bits.

"Luckily, the fat pig farmer had a well-equipped butcher-ing room—lots of shiny, sharp cleavers with big, big blades—

so we were able to eliminate the problem of easy identification." Thomson allowed himself a delicate shudder. "So much blood. Even I didn't expect to have to hose away so much blood. And, luckily, a decent meat grinder and some sausage casing enabled us to get rid of a lot of the smaller bits, the hands, feet. USDA choice, don't you know?"

"More pork sausages Ma!" cried Otis. Thomson smiled indulgently. "The head was too big to pulverize on such short notice. So we found—uh—someone to care for it. The torso was no problem, thanks to you."

"That's when we came in," Sara realized. "You put the 'coffin' out for some stupid tourists to buy."

"Your appearance was unfortunate for all concerned," said Thomson. "You barged in on us before we had a chance to find Die Kugel. And since you insisted on buying the body from me, I thought it expedient to vacate the premises immediately after you left. No telling when those garbage bags would start to leak dwarf."

"For your information, the leaking started on my new dhurrie rug," Sara said snippily.

"Pity."

"But you didn't know what furniture Stoltzfus sold to Bainey," Sam said. "How did you know the dwarf would put the receipt in his family Bible?"

"A little research," Thomson said. "He always kept valuable documents in the Bible. It was a matter of waiting a few days, until I was sure the police hadn't discovered Stoltzfus's disappearance, and then we returned to the scene of the crime, as it were. But the Bible was gone. You wouldn't happen to know anything about that, would you?"

"Sorry," said Sam.

"No matter. We'll take what you've got in the car. It seems a safe bet that you didn't buy that clock because you needed a timepiece to remind you when it's . . . Baby's bed-time."

"You fiend!" Sara shrieked. "What do you know from Baby?"

Thomson smiled. "Cute kid," he said.

From the car seat came the sound of crying.

"I'm keeping score here," Sam said. "We know why you killed Stoltzfus. But why kill Bainey? He didn't have anything to do with this?"

"Who said anything about killing Bainey? The clumsy old bastard was a fool, but harmless." Thomson nodded toward his henchman, who untied the clock from the top of the Rover, and, with a grunt, lugged the cargo to the back of the pickup.

"And I'm afraid you three will have to come with us. Think of it as a family outing. Your last."

"But if you didn't kill Bainey, who did?" Sam desperately wanted to buy time. "We heard on the radio that he was murdered this morning."

"Fascinating," Thomson said. "A good question: Who killed Bainey?"

"Drop 'em."

Merle Otis and Thomson dropped their guns and linked their hands atop their heads. But neither Sam nor Sara, nor Thomson for that matter, could see why.

Then they could. A ferocious little man appeared from behind a parked car. "Calvesi?" said Sam and Sara in unison, for indeed it was the tiny hit man, a .357 Bulldog in his right fist. In his left hand was a small overnight bag.

"Glad to see they let you out for good behavior," Sam said.

"Yeah, must have been all those nice license plates you made," Sara said.

"Shut up."

"Calvesi who?" Thomson said.

"Shut up," Calvesi said again. "All of you shut the fuck up and line up behind the truck. Except the kid. She stays where she is." Which was fortunate, since it would have taken a good ten minutes to disentangle Baby from the car seat.

They lined up behind the truck.

Calvesi pointed the revolver at Sara. "You little bitch," he said. "The husband, now, I don't have anything against him really. It was all business. But you."

"Oh, we had some good times," Sara said. "Come on."

"Oh, please, just one shot, just one. . . . I'd really like to blow your fucking head off," Calvesi confessed, shaking his head. "And I was going to, too. I was going to fix you guys real good. But a guy's got to play the angles. And this god-damn thingie, that's something I'd be stupid to pass up. No sense complicating everything by leaving a trail of brains all over the parking lot."

Calvesi gave a quick bowlegged trot around to the driver's side of the truck, reached up and opened the door. Then he opened his overnight bag, removed a telephone book, and pitched it up, onto the seat.

"Besides," he said, "you got enough troubles, what with the cops after you for killing me and stuffing me in a chest and all. Maybe you'll fry anyway. I hope so, you bitch."

Calvesi climbed up into the truck. "And if you don't get the chair for killing an ex-con, you'll get it for offing that nice pig farmer. Guaranteed."

"How did you know about Bainey?" Sam asked.

"Me? I told you, I'd go to great lengths to ruin your lives."

"You killed Bainey? Just to set us up?"

Calvesi laughed. "Yeah, I killed him. But try convincing the cops that it wasn't you. This is even better than killing you. Maybe you'll see me at the trial. I'll wear a wig and sit in the back, weeping. Everybody will think I'm your mother, wondering where I went wrong."

He turned the key in the ignition.

"My dear friend," said Thomson, "let us not be hasty. You are clearly a shrewd soul indeed to recognize the value of our little object. But what do you propose to do with it?"

"Sell it, Milkface. You got a problem with that?"

"Of course not. I just think you might fetch a better price if you allowed us to market it. . . ."

"Us? You mean you and your buddy?" Calvesi pretended to think for a second. *"Nawww,"* he said at last. "Three's a crowd." He slammed the door. "Nice truck." He rolled up the window and drove off.

Before anybody had time to move or speak, a convoy of Pennsylvania police officers screeched into the parking lot, six cars all together. And before the first cruiser came to a complete stop, a wild-haired woman jumped out of the passenger side and drew her pistol. "Freeze!"

"Thank heavens, the police!" said Thomson. "Quickly, you must stop—"

"Aren't flea markets a little out of your field of expertise, Sara?" asked Detective Sergeant Evelyn Graber, in her best hard-nosed-cop voice. "Looking for a head and hands to match a body?"

"Cute, Graber," said Sara.

"My truck! He stole my truck." Thomson pointed in the direction Calvesi had disappeared.

"I'm never cute when I'm working, and I'm definitely working," said Graber, pulling an official-looking white form out of a notebook she had pressed against her blue down jacket.

"Will you listen to me, please," said Thomson, pulling on Graber's sleeve.

She glared at him. "I am not an officer within your jurisdiction, sir. Please, I'm sure one of these officers behind me would be more than happy to help."

Noonan stepped up and took Thomson aside.

Graber turned back to her prey, and with a ceremonious flick of her wrist, opened the paper form. "I have a warrant here for your arrest, for the murder of one Dominic Calvesi, also known as The Muscle," Graber said, a thin smile playing on her chapped lips. "Let's see here. You have the right to remain silent . . ."

"You just missed him," said Sam.

"You have the right to . . . I beg your pardon?"

"He said, 'You just missed him,'" said Sara. "As in about forty-five seconds ago. He stole the truck that that gentleman is upset about."

"Uh-huh," said Graber, unmoved, but listening.

"Probably if you hightailed it, you might reach him by the time he got to the turnpike."

"But I'd leave right now if I were you. That midget looks like he has a lead foot," Sam said.

Noonan, appearing at Graber's side, barked an order to two officers in a nearby patrol car. "Take a shortcut and head off that midget!" He turned to Sam and Sara. "I've always wanted an excuse to say that," he explained.

Graber was starting to frown. "What midget? What are you talking about?"

"Detective Graber, this is not that difficult," Sam said. "Calvesi has been stalking us for days, probably since we got to Pennsylvania, maybe ever since he got out of jail. He just stole a truck from this man, who happens to be the fellow who murdered the dwarf we found in a chest in our living room."

"You New Yorkers don't do anything easy, do you?" Noonan asked. He gestured to two other officers, who trained their guns on Thomson and Otis. "Just in case you boys felt like edging away in the middle of all this fun," he explained.

"Lieutenant Noonan," Graber blustered. "surely you aren't going to fall for this cockamamy story. Surely you aren't gullible enough to let these two murderers lead you on a wild goose chase."

"Graber, you watch too much bad TV," Sara said.

Graber bristled again, this time at the suggestion that she might get home from work early enough to watch any programs, bad or otherwise.

"Sergeant, we thought you might need a little convincing. Which is why"—Sam pulled a microcassette recorder from under his armpit—"we taped this little interlude here." He rewound the tape for a few seconds, then hit the play button.

". . . why did I kill Stoltzfus? I never met the man. Otis killed him, sort of at my direction," said Thomson's voice. The pale man colored.

Smith appeared from behind an RV parked nearby. "Material evidence. Please be careful with the material evidence." He snatched the tape recorder from Sam's hand, examined it, and then said, "Lieutenant Noonan, I'm Stanley Smith. These two people are my clients. Let's make it clear, in writing, before we leave the scene, that we're turning over a taped confession that exculpates my clients."

Noonan took the tape recorder Smith offered. "I think we can swear out a statement," Noonan said. "No problem."

Thomson spit disgustedly onto the macadam. "You double-crossing . . . reporters," he hissed, hurling the ugliest epithet he knew. "You nosy, busybody reporters."

"I am rubber, you are glue, whatever you say bounces off me and sticks to you," Sara informed him.

"Should be good listening," Noonan said, nodding at the tape. "I suppose you folks will be in the neighborhood for another day or so? I expect the district attorney might want to talk to you about testifying."

"Always glad to cooperate with the law," Sam said. "We're staying at—"

"We know where you're sleeping," Noonan said. "Sergeant Graber took the whole force on a tour."

Graber, speechless, glared from Sam to Noonan to Sam. She couldn't bear to look at Sara.

"Oh, I forgot, did you folks want to file a report on whatever Calvesi stole from you?" Noonan asked.

"*Nyahh,*" Sara said. "It was just a junky old clock we bought at the auction. Would have been more trouble to strip and refinish than it was worth."

"Yeah, I think we'll just mosey back inside. Auction's still going on. Maybe we can pick up another one just like it," Sam said.

"Uh, if you'll excuse us, Lieutenant Noonan, I must have a word with my clients." Smith clamped a hand on each of their arms and steered them out of earshot.

"Have a good day, folks."

But Sam and Sara didn't respond. In fact, they didn't even hear what Noonan had said, their capacity for pleasantries momentarily deadened by the disturbing news Smith was whispering.

"They left?" Sara hissed. "Left? But the plan was—"

"Bought Lot 317, collected it, and left. That's what I came back out here to warn you about." Smith jerked his head toward the back of the parking lot, its rows of cars obscured by the auction house. "Loaded it and drove off. I tried to stop them. They just waved good-bye out the back window."

TWENTY-EIGHT

The second-best gauge of spring's arrival in Chinatown is the riotous display of foods that grocers drag out onto the sidewalks for the inspection of shoppers: crates of knobbed tubers, branches of ginger, and trays of crushed ice, on which flop just-killed carp and mackerel. Sam and Sara emerged from the urine smell of the subway steps, squinting in the sudden sunlight that illuminated the bustle of Canal Street. Baby, riding her father's shoulders, squealed with pleasure at the sight of a dozen mechanical rats, emitting battery-operated squeaks as they scampered around the feet of an industrious entrepreneur on the corner of Mott Street. "Rat souvenir. Five dollar," he called. "Five dollar. Real hair."

"Sweetie, we already have rats at home," Sara reminded Baby as they made their way slowly through the thicket of

Saturday shoppers and hordes of tourists—a group comprising all but the residents of the five boroughs, in Sara's view—whose swelling numbers are the best indicator that winter has receded, welcoming in its place spring and its attendant influx of Long Islanders.

They shoved their way into the Silver Palace, walked up the stationary escalator, and pushed through a throng of regulars who knew it was wise to arrive by eleven to avoid the real rush. At the edge of the cavernous dining room stood what passed for a maître d' in their favorite brunch spot: a short guy in a cheap black suit, who, as usual, was yelling Chinese into a Mister Microphone, indicating to the waiters in this football-field-sized dining room how many people waited in each party.

Sam scanned the room (seating capacity 800 by order of the fire marshal) and spotted Smith waving from a round table under one of the mounted dragon heads. A red eye blinked above him. Baby loved those blinking red eyes, but not as much as her mother did.

Carefully they picked their way among the round tables that seated eight, friends and strangers side by side. The roar of the 800, the sweet, meaty smell of pork buns, the roiling sweep of the place . . . it was good to be home. Of course, had they known then that they shared the same thought, one would have informed the other, "You owe me a Coke," and the requisite ten punches in the arm would have been meted out.

"Wife want pork bun."

Sam flagged a waitress as she trundled past, pushing a steaming metal cart loaded with plates of dim sim.

"Start with shrimp dumplings," he said, signaling for two plates of three.

"You're late," Smith said.

"With good reason," said Sara.

"Oh?"

"Mail call." Sam produced a postcard from the pocket of his blue union work shirt.

"Sam, I thought you were going to bait him with that," Sara said, disappointed.

"Can't wait." Sam flicked the postcard across the table to Smith. A young Chinese couple seated on his other side looked briefly at the card as it flew by, then returned their attention to an appetizing concoction of fried squid, black bean sauce, and lo mein.

Smith looked at the picture first. It showed the inside of a dome, decorated with a faded frieze of the Garden of Eden. "Villa Villoresi," the caption said. "A few kilometers north of Florence, Italy." The attorney grunted and flipped the card over and read aloud:

" 'Dear friends: A relief to bid *ciao* to the tenure tread-mill, thanks to your help. Try not to hold a grudge. We think of you fondly. Jake and Molly.' "

"We must visit," Sara said.

"We must extradite," Smith said. "This is an outrage."

"We must have more tea," Sam said. He signaled to a waiter.

Baby poked the linen tablecloth with one of her plastic chopsticks.

"I must say you're taking this lightly," Smith said, slurping Diet Coke through a straw. "After that mealymouthed academic phony double-crossed us and fled the country with about fifteen million dollars' worth of loot."

"Or only a hundred and fifty thousand dollars. We're not sure Die Kugel even existed," said Sam.

"And now flaunting it by sending a postcard," said Smith.

"Nervy." Sara popped a chopstick laden with sticky rice

and a crunchy shrimp into her mouth. "Notice the Swiss postmark."

"Maybe we should pursue. Been a long time since we tasted any really fine chocolates," Sam mused.

"Well, we weren't the first people he double-crossed," Sara said. "Imagine how Thomson et al. feel—and they're waiting to be tried for murder. It must steam Thomson to sit in his jail cell thinking about how it was Jake all along who thwarted his plans to buy Die Kugle, how it was Jake who got Stoltzfus to up the ante. Old Jake was calling all the shots right from the start, even as he pretended he would help Thomson find Die Kugel after Stoltzfus died. The only thing Jake needed was a couple of schlubs to figure out where the thing was hidden—and tell him."

"Even a hundred and fifty thousand is a nice windfall for a second honeymoon in Europe," said Sam. A woman pushing a cart of wok-sauteed mussels wheeled by. Smith shuddered.

"Let us not forget Calvesi," Smith said.

"Yeah. I wonder how he likes Pennsylvania," said Sam. "I imagine the penitentiary there is a little better than he's used to. I guess your news is almost as good as mine."

"Do tell." Sam sucked a long strand of noodle into his mouth.

"Word around the precinct is that Stavropoulos is being promoted. Seems he solved the last missing piece of the puzzle. After Graber went off the deep end at Dietrich's Auction House, hallucinating and trying to arrest Noonan, they pulled her off the case and assigned Stefan to type up the reports. So he's sitting at his desk—"

"This must have occurred sometime between eleven and eleven-thirty in the morning on an alternate Tuesday if he was actually doing some work at his desk," Sara said.

"—and he's typing and he gets to the part where they find Bainey's body." Smith paused for effect.

His audience put down their chopsticks to signal total attention.

"And he says, you know how he's always coming out with this stuff, he says, 'I wonder why Scarlett wouldn't come out.' And Erbatz, who's on his way in, anyway, to take Stefan out to lunch, says, 'Who's Scarlett?' And Stavropoulos says, 'The pig. The pig never came out of her hut. Usually a big fat sow runs right out to get fed when people are around. So what kept her inside?' "

"What did keep her in the hut?" Sam asked.

"The head. Rather the skull. Turns out that when Thomson was tidying up, he tossed Stoltzfus's head in there. Picked pretty well clean, as you can imagine." Smith bit into a steamed dumpling. "But the dental records were enough."

A waiter bearing a plate of fried ten-ingredient lo mein floated up to the table and set the steaming dish in front of Sara. "Hey, we didn't order this," she said. The unsmiling waiter pointed to a table across the room, and Sam and Sara groaned as they saw the balding, pink, bespectacled head of Max Goldberg nodding graciously. He raised a teacup and saluted them.

Sara whispered, "Did you ever call him back?" Sam shook his head no. Already Goldberg was working his way over to their table.

"So confess, you little monkeys! You miss me, you miss the news biz, and you're ready to beg me for your old jobs back, right?" said Goldberg, slapping Sam on the back and leaning down to smear Sara's makeup with a wet kiss.

"Max, so good to see you," said Sara dully.

"Baby, Baby. Yes sir, she's my baby." Goldberg tried to squeeze Baby's cheek. But the wily infant was too quick for him, feinting to the side as he moved in, and stabbing her pincer fingers at a tuft of the bristly hair inside the King's ear. Goldberg stood up quickly.

"Seriously, guys," he said, "let's talk."

"Seriously, Max," said Sara, "we'd love to."

"When we get back from our next trip," said Sam.

"Trip, what trip?" asked Smith.

"For our next issue," said Sam.

"On chocolates," said Sara.